Stories from the Streets

Mac Mallory

Pen Press

First published in Great Britain by Pen Press

All paper used in the printing of this book has been made from wood grown in managed, sustainable forests.

ISBN: 978-1-78003-439-3

Printed and bound in the UK
Pen Press is an imprint of
Indepenpress Publishing Limited
25 Eastern Place
Brighton
BN2 1GJ

A catalogue record of this book is available from the British Library

Cover design by Jacqueline Abromeit

Stories from the Streets

m. mallory

Author's Notes

This is my attempt at putting on paper just what it was like in the streets of Northern Ireland from the point of view of the ordinary soldier in the late '60s.

After full consideration, I have decided to change names and dates and places as after a quiet period over there and as this long-running problem is in reality nearly on our doorsteps.

Although this book is a work of fiction it is based on fact. The Libyans were sending Arms by the shipload to the I.R.A, but we did not actually deal with them. That was left to the Special Forces and The Royal Navy, and the Libyans never actually landed as I suggested in the McGilligan chapter. Also I was obviously not allowed to go around blowing front doors off with a Carl Gustav. And I don't think it would be fair to the other people taking part in what was happening to publish their names.

Even after all the publicity about Tony Blair solving all the problems over there they have not, and maybe never will, be solved. This business has been going on for over 300 years now, and religion only separates the two factions now. It is more a problem of organised crime and dirty politics.

What follows is a collection of short stories in which I will attempt to show the side of the ordinary soldier doing a far from ordinary job.

We were the early boys; we didn't have Kevlar, or body armour, only nylon flak vests that would deposit copious amounts of nylon into bullet wounds making them far worse than they should ever have been. We had no armoured Land

Rovers, but we still had to face the bombs the bullets and blood.

We didn't have to face the Taliban and the Hill Tribesmen, but we did have to face curly headed IRA brigade commanders, who could turn up at the Bloody Sunday riots carrying a sub-machine gun and after an atrociously expensive inquiry the blame lands on the young soldiers that are in the streets risking their lives on a daily basis. And after all that, he goes on to become a politician. A member of the British Parliament. These soldiers that conveniently got the blame here were 19-year-old kids who reacted in the only way they possibly could when shots were fired and the command and control structure had broken down.

The money spent on this massively expensive inquiry was completely wasted and could have been spent on something sensible like hospitals, or helping the wounded soldiers returning from Afghanistan. Once again, it's a case of the British politician abandoning the young soldiers who have to face the bombs and bullets to correct the mistakes of the aforesaid politicians.

And the casualty lists for Afghanistan are now overtaking the lists of our losses in Northern Ireland.

The worst case I can remember of British politicians making political capital from the blood of British soldiers, was when a Labour politician made his maiden speech in parliament on the back of a young Grenadier Guards captain killed in Ireland on duty with the SAS, running the man down in public when he had just died in the service of his country, and whilst at the same time his family were alive and living in London, is the lowest-of-low blows. But then the best help we got from Whitehall was for these highly paid people to come up with a damned silly yellow card that we were supposed to read before firing back at someone who was firing at us. These were the people who only had to sit behind a desk in Whitehall and we had to face the streets of Northern Ireland.

I've served in Northern Ireland, the Gulf, Cyprus, Aden, or South Yemen as it is now called, where 13-year-old kids thought it was a good idea to throw a hand grenade in the back of a passing British Army lorry, and I've been to various other places. I've been shot at, but luckily I've never been shot. I've had my problems with PTSD (Post-traumatic Stress Disorder) – in a milder form at one stage having hallucinations of Jesus Christ looking through the window at me – but I think the biggest problem facing our brave fighting men is actually the mandarins in Whitehall.

Read on and see if I can actually paint you an accurate picture of what we were facing in the streets of Northern Ireland.

This book is not to be considered anything but a work of fiction. It is definitely not a *Bravo Two Zero* or *The One That Got Away*. But I have to say I did the research for this book the hard way, i.e. in the streets of Londonderry in the late 1960s, carrying a gun and getting shot at quite regularly by the "Black Balaclava Boys".

Things have moved on a lot since those days; some of the people we had to face in the streets are now high-ranking politicians. How things change over the years. But one thing that never changes is the high cost in young lives.

The casualty lists from Northern Ireland are just now being overtaken by the lists for Iraq and Afghanistan. In the book *The Real Bravo Two Zero*, the author makes a very good point when he says that Andy McNab and co. could have done a lot worse if they had been taken by the Provisional IRA, rather than the Iraqi thugs working for Saddam Hussein.

I have to agree with him, if they had been taken by the Black Balaclava Boys they would probably never have survived to write their highly lucrative books.

Acknowledgements

Thanks to Mike Allie and my grandson I.T. Jack, firstly for financial help, then the I.T. help from Jack, without whom this work would never have come to publication.

Thanks to my wife Sylvie for her patience in correcting my Colonial English, and printing the first rough copies for storage.

Also, thanks to Roy the boss for his I.T. help, yes I really am an information technology dinosaur.

The Gurkhas

As far as I know, the Gurkhas were never seconded to Northern Ireland, but I couldn't help thinking what a shock the Black Balaclava Boys would have gotten if they had.

And on reflection when writing this, I couldn't help but think that it would indeed be churlish to write a book on the British Army, albeit a work of fiction, without including the famous "Little Smiley Guys" from Nepal, who after 200 years of glorious service with the British Army they have gained the reputation for being one of the fiercest fighting regiments to have ever served in the British Army.

"Always happy, always smiley, and always up for a fight" should have been their motto.

So I thought it would be fun to throw these guys into the mix, and introduced them in The Marching Season chapter, and then see what adventures we can find for them to follow that up.

One example of their marvellous sense of humour occurred in the middle '60s. Yes, I really am that old.

We were on exercise on Salisbury Plain, the scene of many such adventures that all British soldiers experience at one time or another in their career. After drawing the short straw, I was elected camp sentry, never a good thing when on exercise against the famous "Small Soldiers" from Nepal.

At around three in the morning I heard what sounded like a little kid giggling in the bushes to my front. Knowing that they would only come around in the morning and tell everyone what they had been up to, the big brave sentry, yours truly, went to investigate and promptly went ass over tip in the mud, rifle and all.

When we say that these little guys virtually turn into a ghost at night in the field, it is not that much of an exaggeration. The little fellow had managed to creep up to me in the dark and tie my bootlaces together without me knowing it.

Now you might say that this is an indication of how bad my field craft at night was at that time, but rest assured, it is an indication of how good theirs is.

Anyway, although placing them in the Province is an act of artistic licence on my part, let's see what adventure we can find for them as we go along.

Prologue

The two boys were absolutely terrified; they both bore the scars on their backs from the brass-tipped army swagger stick, wielded by their sadistic father, Colonel Mallory. Mac, the oldest, could have lived with the beatings and the pain of his bleeding back, but what he could not live with were the screams and tears from his younger brother, and even on occasion from this mother.

His mother was not a strong woman, and she was completely under the spell of the sadistic martinet that was his father.

After a bad session, his younger brother Harry would hide under his bed whimpering and crying like a little puppy, and Mac would have to spend long hours, persuading the younger boy to come out from under the bed so that he could administer first aid, cleaning and disinfecting the cuts and abrasions so that they wouldn't become infected.

Then the ice-cold anger would turn inwards, where it would fester and percolate. No young man should ever have to regard his father with this kind of cold hatred, but young Mallory did.

And this hatred was made worse, if that was possible, when he had to tend the same wounds on his mother's back while she was quietly sobbing and flinching every time he touched an open wound with the cotton buds soaked in alcohol. And all the while it was playing on his mind, that if he didn't leave home soon, he would end up killing his own father, with all the repercussions and damage that would bring to a boy's mind.

He was only just finished with tending his mother's wounds when the front door crashed open and the drunk and swaggering little sadist stood there, swaying back and forth.

"What are you looking at?" he slurred, but instead of cowering under the bed, the boy faced up to his fears and looked him straight in the eye.

"I'm looking at something that I would normally scrape off the bottom of my shoe," the boy said quietly and coldly.

The swagger stick came up sharply to cut him across the face, but this time the boy didn't even flinch. The colonel looked the boy in the eye and what he saw looking back at him stopped him cold. He suddenly found that he was looking death in the eye, and he was frozen by the sudden terror that struck him straight in the guts.

He suddenly lowered the stick and stepped back. Then he started to bluster. "Right, you little bastard, do you think you can stand up to me? I'm going to make arrangements for you to go to West Point, and I'm going to do it tomorrow. They will beat some respect and discipline into you."

The boy looked him straight in the eye and smiled coldly. "I'm not going to West Point or anywhere else for you, and if you lay your hands on Harry or my mother again, I'll kill you!"

The colonel said shakily, "If you're going to live in my house you will do as I say," he spluttered.

"Well then, you know the answer to that, Colonel," and once more the little sadist looked into his son's eyes and he could only see death looking back at him.

The next day while the colonel was at his desk, Mac bundled his mother and brother onto a train heading for Vancouver, where she had relatives who would look after her and Harry.

"Come with us, Mac," she pleaded.

"No," he said slowly. "I have to get as far away from him as I can, or I'll end up killing him, and what would that do to us?"

The train that he did board wasn't going north, it was going east. Mac found that all the time his mother and brother were safe from his sadistic father; he could look after himself quite well. He was a big strapping lad and he worked his way towards the east coast, turning his hand to any job that came his way. He worked on cattle ranches, on construction jobs and taxi driving.

He found that he could happily adapt to whatever he had to do to make a buck. He was a happy, healthy, growing young man with an appetite like a horse and he seemed to grow bigger week by week.

He even found the time to phone his father and as soon as the little bully came on the line he started ranting and raving. Mac let him carry on for a couple of minutes, then he brought him up short with a grated, "Shut up, you evil old man." And when there was finally silence on the end of the phone, he snarled, "I want nothing from you. I'll live my own life now, and if you ever go anywhere near my mother or Harry again, I will come back and kill you. Just leave them alone," and the cold voice on the end of the line left the colonel in no doubt that the boy would do just that.

Mac moved from one job to another quite happily because the last thing he wanted to do was to settle down and have the hated old man find him, although it was the colonel who would come off worse if they were ever to meet again.

Mac checked on his mother and Harry frequently and he was happy that they were thriving. Harry was going to school in Vancouver and his mother was working in a restaurant there. She was never going to make a fortune, but they were making a living. Mac spoke frequently to his Uncle Danny, who was looking after them there, and he was just happy that they were safe and out of his father's clutches.

Mac settled happily into a life on the road. It was a hard, hard life that gradually turned him into a hard, hard man. He worked as a bouncer in some of the roughest road-houses on the Eastern Seaboard. There were times when the boy's response to the would-be hard men that invaded these road-houses was too much even for the gangsters that ran these places. When the police got tired of turning up to answer a 911 call only to find that the troublemakers were already on the ground waiting for an ambulance to take them to hospital, he would once more have to move on to another job, or spend time in a country jail. Still, all this experience would stand him in good stead for the job he would eventually end up doing.

His travels took him ever onwards and ever closer to the East Coast, until he ended up on Prince Edward Island, where it made sense to him to sign on to a freighter heading for Liverpool in England. And like everything else he turned his hand to, Mac made a good sailor, still eating like a horse and growing all the time.

When they put into Liverpool, the captain happily paid him up and asked him to sign on for the return journey, but the last thing he wanted to do was to go back to America. So he collected his pay and wandered the Liverpool streets, not really caring where he was going, as long as he wasn't going back to the colonel's world. In fact, the little sadist was now a one-star general, not that it would cut any ice with Mac, if he had known, he just wanted to keep on going away from his father.

Mac was sitting in a dingy back street bar nursing a pint of warm beer when he was approached by a local wide boy.

"Can I buy you a drink, Yank?" he said.

"Yeah, why not?" said Mac, his mind far away with his mother and brother in Vancouver. As the drink went agreeably down, the wide boy got straight down to business.

"Ok, Yank, do you want to make some easy money?"

"It depends on what I have to do to earn it," said Mac, unsuspectingly.

"Easy peasy," said the wide boy. "These people I work for sometimes loan some money to a family here in town, and they're not keeping up with the payments, so we need to put the frighteners on them!"

That statement brought Mac up short.

"Frighteners?" he asked quietly.

"Yeah," said the wide boy with far too much confidence, not paying enough attention to the look on Mac's face. "We go in and scare them into paying up, easy peasy!"

Already the bad memories of his father putting "the frighteners" on his mother and brother were flooding back.

"Let's go out the back and you can give me all the details."

When Mac came back into the bar, the barman said, "Where's your friend, Mac?"

"Not my friend, but he had to go," said Mac, and with that he finished his drink and left the bar.

"Yanks," shrugged the barman, then thought no more of it. When he went out into the alley to take the rubbish out at closing time, he found the wide boy laying in the skip moaning. Both of his arms were broken, his eyes were swollen shut, and when they got him to hospital, all he could do was moan about a crazy Yank that said, "How's this for putting the frighteners on?"

As he wandered the streets of Liverpool carrying his meagre belongings in a cheap suitcase, he suddenly spotted an army recruiting office, where he was welcomed with open arms. As the recruiting sergeant went into overdrive and his spiel was assaulting Mac's ears, Mac suddenly thought, *why the hell not?* They would pay him a wage, give him a bunk, give him four squares a day, and put a gun in his hands. Hell, this was the army, but it was a million miles away from his father's army. He really couldn't find a better place to hide, no matter how hard he tried. So he signed on the dotted line, and the good thing about the

British Army was that they didn't care where you came from, they took people from all over the world. Hell, one of their most famous units was made up from the fierce mountain warriors from Nepal.

Mac took to his army training like a duck to water; he loved the weapon training, the fitness training and the survival training, but he really had no stomach for the spit and polish "bullshit" training.

After the first 12 weeks' training was finished, they were allowed out on the town for a weekend of drink and debauchery, but they had to wear uniform, which in itself didn't bode well for things to come. Mac and three of his friends were settled in the third floor bar in the Aldershot NAAFI, and so far things were going smoothly, until around 10.30 a half-dozen parachute regiment guys staggered into the bar.

"Look out, boys, things could get a bit lively now!" grinned Mac wryly, and it didn't take long for things to kick off. When the massive Wurlitzer jukebox went sailing out of the window, Mac laughed and shouted over the din, "Only one thing for it now, guys!"

"What, do we fight?" shouted one of the younger, more inexperienced of the company excitedly.

"Hell no," laughed Mac. "Do you want to spend the night in hospital then be taken back to camp in chains? It's time for a tactical withdrawal, hats off, under the table and head for the door!"

Finally, three breathless young squaddies and one slightly older Yank made it to the door in fits of giggles and headed out to find a much quieter watering hole.

It wasn't long before Mac finished his basic training and was on his way to his first active service posting, which happened to be the hotspot of the late '60s, Northern Ireland, and he was soon settled into The Sailor's Rest in Londonderry. Now came the serious business!

Contents

Chapter One

Two Kinds of Fear (the Buzz)

They always said that the American Army has a drug problem and the British Army has a drink problem. But there was always another way to get high, on a pure adrenalin overdose.

The IEDs or roadside bombs that caused the highest percentage of casualties in Northern Ireland, and still are in Afghanistan, used to scare the living shit out of us in Ireland and probably still do in "The Stan", as the boys call it.

Don't get me wrong, anyone who says their asshole doesn't pucker when the bullets zip close overhead is a damned liar. You stay alive longer with that fear in your mind, but it's a different kind of fear.

The fear of the IEDs is an evil, crawling thing. The fear of bullets zipping close overhead is a different thing, it keeps you alive and gives you a pure adrenalin high that is addictive, and some of the young lads say is better than sex, but I wouldn't go that far. But I have to say it not only keeps you alive, it also makes you feel alive. I had experienced both the crawling, evil, debilitating fear of the IEDs and the clean adrenalin-filled fear of the close-up fire-fight.

I was rostered for a foot patrol with Sergeant Gerry Anderson, and a full section of infantry, on a clear, sunny Saturday morning in July.

Gerry was patrol commander, with Corporal Tim Riley and six privates, including me. We were tasked with a walkabout from "The Rest" down to the town square and up to the top of William Street and back down to The Rest. Just a weekend stroll really, just to remind the locals that we were in charge and to invite the local bad boys to take a potshot at us if they were so inclined.

The drill was to have half the section on one side of the road with Gerry in charge, and the other half section on the other side with Tim in charge. That way you could move forward, taking cover in doorways and you could cover the other half section, while engaging any nasties on the upper floors, on the other side of the street.

We were doing our thing, working our way down and around the square, before we had to take a stroll up William Street and back down again. Gerry couldn't resist a dig as we worked our way from doorway to doorway.

"Shit, Yank, how come you're still awake?"

"Hell, Sarge, I've got to stay awake to look after you!"

I had a reputation with these boys, if I didn't need to be awake to shoot someone, I was usually asleep.

As we worked our way from door to door, things suddenly went noisy. Gerry was a few paces in front of me when suddenly there was the familiar crackle of small arms' fire.

I swear, the people in this town must know that sound as well as we do by now. Gerry hit the ground as quickly as me when the AK47 rounds stitched across the brickwork just above our heads.

As the masonry dust showered down on us, Gerry let go with a high-pitched excited laugh.

"Shit, Yank, isn't this just as good as a three-day pass in Bangkok with a pocket full of money?"

"Well, Sarge," I said, as I studied the windows across the road from us, "I've never been to Bangkok but I think I know what you mean!" I was still watching the upper windows across the road from us.

Then I saw a rifle barrel sticking out of a window, and I straight away emptied a 20-round magazine into it.

"You get him, Mac?"

"Yeah, I think so, but we'll still have to go in and check it out!"

"Right," he said. "I'm number one, your number two, Mac." Then he shouted out to the rest of the section. "Stephens and Anderson follow me and Mac. You know the drill, we've done it hundreds of times before. The rest of you cover us when we go in!"

When the other two formed up behind us, he looked at me and smiled. "Are you up for this, Yank?"

"Course I am, Sarge. I don't agree that this shit is better than sex but it runs a close second!"

"Right, Yank," he laughed. "Got the sledgehammer?" Stephens came up and gave it to me. I swapped my SLR for the radio operator's SMG, as the number two; the short gun would do me more good than the long gun.

I looked at Gerry. "You ready, Sarge?" He nodded, and then I hit the door with the sledgehammer. As the door slammed back I dropped the sledge and stepped back for Gerry to go in first.

As he went in he ducked low and moved to the left, I followed him and automatically went to the right. So far so good, we were in and no one was shooting at us.

Gerry signalled for Stephens and Perry to clear the upper floors while we cleared the ground floor and the garden, and then looked to the basement. I'd had bad experiences with basements before, but Gerry had gone through the front door first, so the basement was down to me.

I looked at Gerry, then I moved into position and kicked in the door, nothing happened. Once more I looked at Gerry and as I started down the stairs he moved into position to cover me.

But it was all quiet down there; I only found old tins of paint and assorted basement things. When I got back upstairs I said to Gerry, "All clear down there, Sarge."

3

Stephens and Perry came downstairs. Stephens shrugged, "Nothing. Sarge. Only the one Mac got, and he was still holding his AK. Hell, Sarge, you know if we walk around these streets long enough somebody will eventually work up the gumption to have a pop at us!"

"Well," laughed Gerry, "you know we've got to keep the natives on their toes!"

With that, he got on the radio to call in the meat wagon to clear up the mess we had left, and when they arrived we moved out to carry on with our patrol.

We'd done the town square and now it was time for my favourite road. Up till now we'd had so much trouble in that road it was becoming like a second home to us.

We started to make our way up William Street with a great deal of caution, moving from doorway to doorway, leapfrogging our way.

Everything seemed to be quiet but one thing we had learned about this town was that appearances were deceiving. If everything looked quiet, we all knew it probably wasn't.

But this time we were wrong, we actually made it up to the top of the road and back down to The Rest without further incident.

Later on in the canteen after we had cleaned our weapons and Gerry was in with Webber and Parker working on his report, the boys were drinking their tea and I was working on my second coke. I had a chance to reflect on the two kinds of fear. The evil, crawling, diseased fear of the IEDs that we had experienced on our last trip to McGilligan, and the clean adrenalin-high-inducing fear of the close-up fire-fight, which could keep you alive, and took you hours to come down from.

Chapter Two

A Bad Saturday Night in Derry

They normally talk about a bad Saturday night in Belfast, but we also had our share of bad Saturday nights in Londonderry. Shots fired, blood on the streets, bombs going off, fires started by petrol bombs. Rubber bullets and barricades were the stuff of nightmares, but all part of the job when we were in the British Army.

We were in the streets and we were expecting a bad night. Dana, a local girl, had won the Eurovision Song Contest and the boys would be in the streets tonight, their way of celebrating.

We were out in the streets in force and I had the luck to be rostered as company driver that night. When Dana arrived at the station she made a speech to the boys, telling them not to cause any trouble, and for everyone to go home quietly.

Well, of course, this was like a red rag to a bull for the hard men of the IRA. After she had gone home, the tension was rising and you could have cut the air with a knife. The boys were gathering on the street corners and the jungle drums were beating; the tension was in the night air.

About 2300 hours the radios started to crackle and we were off. The night sky was lit up by explosions and the crackle of small arms could be heard all over the city.

We got the call about 2330; we were standing by at the police station in the main square. Then came the shout I was expecting; a bellow rocked the corridor and it was coming from the company Sgt. Major.

"Come on, Mac, you lazy old Yank. I need a taxi and you're elected."

It was Sergeant Major Clint Webber, 300lbs of big, hard, noisy warrant officer, who liked the red tape and the "bullshit", as we called it in the army.

"Come on, Mac, you lazy old Yankee bastard, get a move on. There's a young second lieutenant up at the Rosemount School with Number Two Platoon and we've got to go up and give him some backbone."

Well, I saddled up and got my Land Rover ready; SLR in the rack behind the seats and I had four extra 20-round magazines on the dash and a 20-round magazine of 7.62 could sort out lots of problems.

When Webber jumped in the wagon he was carrying a Sterling with extra magazines, and he was bellowing, "Come on, you old bugger, let's get moving."

Well, shit, I thought, just because I'm the oldest man in the company there's no need to labour the point.

They pulled back the barricades at the bottom of William Street and I started going through. At the bottom of William Street coming up from the main square, the road bears around to the right, and from the bottom we couldn't see what they had waiting for us. As I crept around the corner I saw our reception committee; they had 45-gallon drums strung with "Dannert" wire (barbed wire) right across the road.

Webber said to me, "You're not going to stop, are you?"

Well, there was no time to even think about that, we had seen what these crowds could do when they got going. Even with my rifle in the cab I wouldn't have even had time to get to it. When I hit the barricade I was doing about 50mph and I wasn't going to be stopping for anything.

There was a sound like extra-large hailstones in the worst hailstorm you can imagine, as the stones hit my wagon, and luckily I was wearing driving gloves because I had to punch out what was left of my windscreen. I hit the barricade right between two 45-gallon drums with a loud bang. The drums bounced away and I was dragging barbed wire behind me.

One fool picked entirely the wrong time to run in front of me with a lit petrol bomb, ready to throw it at my wagon, and he went under the front and into the wire I was dragging. Unlucky for him he still had the petrol bomb in his hand at the time, and when his body came loose from the wire he wasn't only hamburger, he was burning hamburger. But I was too busy manoeuvring through the barricades our boys had thrown across William Street at the junction at the top of the road.

When our little convoy had parked up behind the hastily returned barricades, Webber went off to sort out the boy officer, and I started checking my wagon over for damage. Every bit of glass would need to be replaced and there were dents all down the driver's side from all the stones and I would have to hose all the blood off the front of the wagon in the morning.

While I was checking my taxi over, the doctor walked up to me and announced that he wouldn't be following me anywhere ever again.

"What's the problem, Doc?" I said. "At least I cleared the barricades for you."

"Yeah," he laughed, "you cleared the barricades for me, all right. Come and have a look."

My Land Rover was in a bad state with all the damage, but his was worse. His had 7.62 bullet holes down the side and through the driver's door, just in front of where his chest would have been. I had stirred the boys up by running their barricade; my wagon got stoned but I woke up the guy with the AK47 and the doc copped it coming through right behind me.

Just another bad Saturday night in Derry. Luckily we didn't lose anyone that night, but the guy with the petrol bomb wasn't so lucky.

My predominate memory of that night isn't the crackle of small arms' fire, not the boom of the bombs going off, not the fear and the adrenalin that floated on the night, but it is and always will be the sickly sweet smell of human flesh burning.

In the morning, after we had cleared up all the mess the boys had made the night before, Webber came to find me to let me know that the body of the man I had left in William Street, bleeding and burning, had turned up in the local morgue.

But in the cold light of day the body in the morgue was there because he was trying to kill me or one of my mates, so that Saturday night wasn't going to send me rushing to the nearest therapist.

Chapter Three

Just Another Bad Night in the Streets

By 2000 hours the tension was electric; small arms' fire was crackling all over the city, punctuated by loud explosions, the whole company was already committed and it was turning out to be another bad night in the streets.

Parker had number one platoon deployed in the square, number two was up at Rosemount and number three was mobile, answering emergency calls as they came in with increasing frequency, and we had three men high up on the Old Derry Wall covering our backs.

We were still not up to full-scale alert, no skid lids yet; you could always tell when things were getting out of hand when the order came around to don steel helmets.

As the crackle of small arms' fire increased, we could tell the boys were working themselves up to a full frenzy. They didn't care if they hurt their own people or us soldiers in the streets as long as they were hurting someone and getting the publicity that they sorely craved.

I was with the arrest squad, taking the boys back to the local nick when our heavies arrested them and brought them back to us behind the barricades.

Harry Phelps was paired up with me, and we had just delivered an indignant soldier of the revolution to his accommodation for the night, and we were on our way back to the barricades to collect our next customer, when I happened to glance up at the Old Derry Wall.

A swarm of Black Balaclava Boys were in the process of overpowering our three men up on the wall. Jesus, I thought, why don't they fire their weapons? I shouted to Harry, "Look up on the wall!" Shit, our boys were going down.

I looked around for Webber, but he was concentrating on the snatch squad and their operations out in front of the barricades. I had to make a decision and do it fast and there was only one way to attract the big guy's attention. I fired three times quickly in the air, gunfire behind him was sure to attract his attention.

He looked back towards me, and I pointed up onto the wall. He took in the situation at a glance, and then he grabbed the two men nearest to him, and motioned to me and Harry to follow him up onto the wall.

When we arrived up on top we found two men unconscious and bleeding profusely from head wounds. Their weapons were missing and the Balaclava Boys were moving off along the wall, dragging our third man along with them. They had obviously decided to take a hostage and we all knew what would happen to that boy if we ever let them get away.

Webber delegated one man to stay and look after the men on the ground and led the rest of us off in hot pursuit of the Balaclava Boys and their prisoner.

We moved off along the wall as rapidly as we could, after all, we really didn't want to blunder into an ambush at this point, but at the same time we couldn't afford to lose sight of them or our man would never be coming home again.

As we followed them along the old wall, they came to the next set of stairs and bundled our boy down none too gently, in other words they threw him down head first. This brought a rumble of dissent from the big guy in front and I thought, pity any of the Balaclava Boys that fell into his hands tonight.

We followed them down into the streets, expecting at any time to start taking fire from the captured SLRs. As I said before, we had no Kevlar body armour at that time so if anyone took a high-velocity round from an SLR, they would quite possibly not be going home with the rest of us, or they would be going home minus an arm or leg as these rifles took no prisoners; a hit centre body mass was invariably fatal and a hit on an arm or leg meant the loss of that limb.

As we followed them down the stairs we saw them dive into a house at the bottom. We now knew that if we didn't engage in some nifty house-to-house immediately we would most certainly lose our man.

Webber was the first to the door with the rest of us in close pursuit. He hit the door like a runaway bulldozer, and the door had no chance. The big guy was the first one inside with me right behind him; we had to keep moving, if our advance ever ran out of steam our man was finished.

As I came through the door behind him I saw a gunman on the first floor drawing a bead on Webber, so I put two quick rounds into his chest. The effect at that range was devastating; he flew backwards hitting the passage wall and leaving a blood trail as he slid down.

I knew we didn't have to worry about him anymore, so I motioned to the man behind me to go up and secure the stolen SLR, and I moved on into the house covering Webber's back, as he was already heading for the back door with me in close pursuit.

As we piled through into the garden, there was a loud crack, and a lump of house brick right beside my head exploded, as another of the Balaclava Boys had his try with another SLR. He should have kept running, because he immediately caught a burst of 9mm from Webber's Sterling that shredded his ribs, flinging him in a haze of pink spray. Two down, one more SLR to recover.

The remaining Balaclava Boys were still trying to drag our man to the back gate and another double tap left one more of the boys lying on the ground, and we had recovered SLR number three.

Suddenly they had had enough and the remaining two soldiers of the revolution decided that discretion was definitely the better part of valour and they disappeared up the back alley – game over.

We collected our boy and this was definitely his lucky night. The butcher's bill on our side was quite light and he was definitely a lucky boy; a broken arm, severe bruising and bleeding, but he was still alive and he had no holes in him.

All Webber said, with an accompanying glare, was "bugger the yellow card, the next time you are in a situation like that, fire your bloody weapon. Shoot the bastards." And by the look on the boy's face I was sure he had learned his lesson.

It was time for us to beat a hasty retreat as we were well out on a limb there. Webber looked at me and growled, "Look after him, Mac. Let's get the hell out of here."

As we made our way back onto the wall and headed back for the square, we were watching our backs all the way, this was definitely not the time to run into an ambush.

We were lucky that night, we had got our man back, albeit bruised and bleeding, and we had also recovered the three stolen SLRs, and I can assure you that things didn't often go that well.

When we got back to the square we found the sentries on the wall had been reinforced; they were ten strong now and really glad to see us back with our man. They had a sergeant with them now, who had a quick conference with Webber, and then we took our boy back down to the ambulance waiting in the square. The riot had run out of steam now and the boys were in the process of cleaning up the mess, a task that always fell to us when the rioters had gone home to bed.

Parker wanted to know where we had been and Webber just grinned and said, "Leave this to me, Mac."

So another bad night in the streets came to an end, and we had come out of it pretty well all things considered. We had three men in hospital, battered and bruised, but none of them had any holes in them and at least three of the Balaclava Boys would not be facing us in the streets again.

Chapter Four

Roadside Bombs

Nowadays in Afghanistan, the cause of probably more than 90% of British Army casualties are the IEDs – the improvised explosive devices – or as we called them back in the '60s in Northern Ireland, roadside bombs.

They were also the cause of a high percentage of British Army casualties in the Province, whether they were remotely detonated by Dikkers, who laid up and waited for a vehicle to drive by, or were detonated by driving over pressure pads in the road.

Every time we set out on a mobile or foot patrol, we knew we ran the risk of coming up against one of these cowardly devices.

In the case of a pressure pad detonation, we knew it would be the lead vehicle, the first one into the ambush, that was going to take the hit. In the case of a remote detonation, it was more or less a lottery; they could pick whatever vehicle they wished to hit.

Such was the case on a bright sunny Saturday morning when we set off on our way back to McGilligan Camp for our R&R – rest and recuperation in army parlance. That morning they decided to set us up for the double whammy, meaning they had a pressure pad device in the road to take out the first vehicle in line, and this day the boys were taking orders from a real smart-ass.

He decided to put a remote device further back in the road, so they could take out the first vehicle with the pressure plate device, then the last in line with the remote device, it turned out to be a very expensive day for us.

We had just crossed over the Craigavon Bridge and started up the hill on the other side. The lead Land Rover hit the pressure plates and the front end disappeared in an orange gout of flame. The vehicle flipped over on its back before the rumbling explosion had died away.

Webber and I were fourth wagon back in line with two privates in the back. Shit, I thought, there was a sergeant, a driver and two privates in the wagon that had just gone up in flames. The day was starting badly and steadily getting worse.

"Jesus, Mac, was that pressure plates or remote?"

"I don't know, sir, but first vehicle in line, probably pressure plates."

Then we found out just what this day was going to cost us. The last vehicle in line erupted in an orange flash and a rumbling explosion. Shit! First and last vehicles, we were boxed in and getting creamed.

"Jesus, Mac," moaned Webber. "That three-tonner had a driver, an officer and a full section of infantry on it." Now we were really in the shit!

Webber was on the radio calling for a couple of Pigs to come up and give the lead Land Rover some cover and run interference for the doc, so he could get in close and see if anyone was alive in the lead wagon.

The Pigs rumbled in, blocking views of the brewing Land Rover and we pulled up near the front of the line, preparing to take over the lead, when we had cleared up the mess.

As soon as we slammed to a halt, I jumped out, taking my SLR. The boy in the back with the GPMG threw it over the framework; he had clearance as we had stripped off the canvas cover before leaving The Rest.

"Were to, Mac?" he shouted.

"Look to the upper floors of the houses across the street," I shouted.

The boy was good; he immediately started tracking his Gimpy back and forth, covering the second and third floor windows.

Webber still had the radio in his hand, calling for the QRF (Quick Reaction Force and Air Support).

"What are you doing, Mac?" he shouted, as I made my way behind the Land Rover to the safest place, behind the front wheel and the engine block. On the way around I dragged my old favourite.

"I'm just getting the flash bang ready, sir," I said as he tumbled out of the front seat and joined me in the safe place.

I was unlimbering my Carl Gustav that had served us so well up at the Rosemount School, where we had sadly lost Dick Shelley.

"I'm thinking they've taken out the lead vehicle with a pressure plate bomb and our tail-end Charlie with a remote, now what do you think comes next?"

"Shit!" he said. "An RPG in the middle of the convoy."

"Yeah, and it's going to come from the upper floor of one of those houses across the road!"

As we were talking, my eyes were roving up and down the street looking at those windows. But it was the GPMG gunner in the back of my wagon that spotted it first; this boy was good.

"Look out, Mac. Second floor window, three houses to your right. Contact, contact! RPG in the upper floor window!" And with that he let fly with a full belt of 7.62.

I saw his target at the same time as Webber did and I immediately sent an HE round through the offending window and Webber joined in with a full magazine from my SLR that I had left propped up beside the Land Rover.

The window disappeared in a gout of orange flame and a shower of masonry dust.

But not before we heard the hauntingly familiar whoosh and thump, followed by the rumbling explosion of the RPG taking out another one of our vehicles. God, I had been too slow. This was really going to be an expensive day for us.

The two big ugly Pigs that Webber had called for finally rolled into position, doing their job and blocking views of the doc doing his job checking out the wreck for survivors.

"Not your fault, Mac," rumbled Webber. "You had the right idea."

I reloaded my flash bang, getting it ready; I knew we were not out of the shit yet.

Just then a middle-aged woman staggered out of the house that I had just re-arranged on the second floor.

She came straight across the road toward me screaming about British Army murderers killing her son.

"Oh, shit," moaned Webber. "We don't need this."

Her son had fired the RPG from her second-story window, taking out another Land Rover and its crew in the middle of our convoy, but we were tagged as murderers, because we fired back when he shot at us.

I have to admit I lost it then, probably for the first time since I had been in the Province. I lost it 100%.

Webber saw the look on my face and stepped in straight away!

"Come on, Mac, she's just lost her son. She's not really responsible for her actions right now!"

Normally I would never have argued with this big shit, who was probably the only personal friend I had in the country. But this time I had lost it completely. I sidestepped the big bugger, I knew I would never get past if I tried to match strength and move him out of the way. Then I approached the screaming woman, my weapons completely forgotten, something which should never happen at that time and place. I could not help myself and I did something I would never normally do, I grabbed her by the scruff of the neck, and pushed her closer to the still burning Land Rover and men.

Webber was close behind me, this time not giving me orders, just trying to calm me down.

"Come on, Mac, let it go. She's just lost her son."

But I couldn't let it go; I pushed her closer to the burning Land Rover and growled in her ear, "Do you smell that? What do you think that smell is? That's what the natives in Borneo call 'long pig'. It's the smell of roast pork and it's the smell of burning men. Burning men who have families in England, who have wives and children in England. And the smell in your nostrils is the smell of those men burning, because your son decided he would like to play with a rocket propelled grenade. Did you really think we wouldn't shoot back at him?"

And then, before I could do something I would regret for a very long time, a very large sergeant major walked up behind me and smothered me with his bulk, picked me up and deposited me ten yards along the road. When I turned around the woman had gone and it was just me and the big guy again.

"Come on, Mac," he growled. "This is our job and we got the shitty end of the stick today. But our turn will come, you know that."

"Shit, you'd better believe it, boss. But now comes the hard part, cleaning up the mess and working out the butcher's bill, as Parker says."

We lost two men in the leading vehicle and two went to the burns unit at East Grinstead.

Although I was too slow with the flash bang to stop the RPG from firing, luckily the alert GPMG gunner in the back of my Land Rover made him miss his target, or the score would have been a lot worse.

The worst result was Tail-end Charlie, the three-tonner at the back of the line.

We lost the driver and the Rupert that was riding in the front and one of the section riding in the back. The rest of the section ended up back at East Grinstead, also in the burns unit. As I said, this was to be a very expensive day for us.

Finally the doc was finished, and then the meat wagon came up to clear our boys out. Then it was the turn of the engineers to clear out the burnt-out vehicles.

And when we finally got under way again, Webber and I were at the head of our sad sorry convoy. We had taken one of the worst hits in the history of our Regiment.

As we rolled off, I realized we were now in the most vulnerable position at the head of the convoy. But then I thought, are we really in the worst position, after all we could be tail-end Charlie.

We eventually got to McGilligan, after a long, apprehensive journey, and we were worn out, pissed off and thinking of looking for another job.

I went to my room and dumped my gear, then went looking for food at the cookhouse. I still didn't know if I was hungry or not after the day we'd had, but trying to operate on an empty stomach was definitely not the way to go in this man's army.

I locked all of my extra weapons away and headed for the cookhouse with my SLR slung over my shoulder. Although the brass said we were in a police action, they, as usual, didn't know what was going on. It was really a war zone and we were armed at all times.

As I got in line for my food, I nodded to the QMSM, Smudger Smith, who was supervising the serving of the evening meal. I picked up my tray and eating irons and moved on to the first tray of food, which just happened to have standing behind it Corporal George Garry, the greasy, spotty oik who I wouldn't let in my house clearance team on the Night of the Pigs. In the British Army if you can't shoot or march they make you up to a corporal and assign you to the cookhouse. Thank God that for every reject that ends up in the cookhouse, there is a good cook already there to make up for it, otherwise soldiers would starve to death.

Anyway, this dickhead still hadn't forgotten me refusing to take him into the house with me and the boys still ribbed him about it. Straight away he made the mistake of smirking and chuckling, "Hell, Mac, I thought you boys were good, but, oh dear, it turns out that you're not so good after all."

Normally I would have ignored him, but not tonight. Wrong time for a wind up.

I said, "What's for dinner, asshole" and he had the nerve to laugh at me and say, "Roast pork, you Yankee bastard."

The QMSM heard him and immediately started towards us, fearing the worst, and he was right. If I said things erupted in the cookhouse, that would really be an understatement.

When I had bounced his head off the hotplate a few times and finished up drowning him in a tray of hot peas, the cookhouse was in an uproar and all the boys were cheering me on.

By the time the QMSM had removed my hand from the back of the silly corporal's head, the MPs were at the door.

Smudger said, "Okay, Mac, we really don't need the MPs, do we?"

I said, "Okay, boss," and turned to walk out the door and he waved the MPs away.

When I was on my way out, he shouted after me, "Where you going, Mac?"

I said, "Don't worry, sir. I'm on my way to the NAAFI bar to start work on a massive hangover."

He chuckled. "Okay, son. But let me check your weapon into the armoury. You don't need it where you're going."

I have to admit I was quite numb when I handed my SLR to him and he said, "Come on, son, you know it makes sense."

I was in the bar working on my third pint with a large vodka chaser when the big shit wandered in.

I said, "You're in the wrong bar, sir."

Webber said, "I'm never in the wrong bar, Mac," as he called the barman over. "Same again for him and I'll have a hit on that as well."

I said, "Did Smudger send you over to check up on me?"

He grinned and said there were some rumours going around that I was causing trouble in the cookhouse.

We sat there quietly until the drinks came, and the big bugger drained half of his in one go.

"Shit," he sighed, "that takes the knots out of your nerves. That was a rough one today, Mac. I thought you were going to lose it for a minute there."

I said, "Yeah, sorry, sir. It's only that we lose men, good soldiers and family men, and the civilians and the newspapers don't bat an eyelid. Then some little scrote will play with fire and explosives and get the short end of the stick and it's all down to us. They say we use too much force and call us murderers, it just pisses me off. What a crock of shit."

"Yeah, well, it goes with the territory, old friend, and like I said before, I wouldn't want you to get pissed off with me. Come on, I've checked out the duty rosters and neither one of us has duty tomorrow so let's get on with building up a huge hangover. And while we're at it we can give those MPs some stick." And then he let go with that rumbling laugh again. Hell, I couldn't stay pissed off with him around and in this mood. I called the barman over to hit us again.

About an hour later Smudger came in and when he saw us at the bar he came over with a big grin on his face.

"Are we going to have trouble with you two reprobates tonight?"

Webber let out his rumbling laugh again and said, "No, you won't need the MPs, but other than that we can't make any promises. Are you going to have a drink with us, or what?"

"Shit," said Smudger. "I don't think I'd be safe with you two buggers. But you have a good night and enjoy yourselves."

And that's exactly what we did!

Chapter Five

McGilligan

Any soldier that served in Northern Ireland in what was euphemistically called "The Troubles", in the Londonderry area, knows all about "The Sailor's Rest" and "McGilligan Camp".

The Rest, as we called it, was our base when we were in the streets of Derry, and although it was only a shitty old merchant sailors' mission, it was like The Ritz compared to the railway sheds that we called home when we first went to the Province. Open to the elements in the front and the back-end of the sheds, we might just as well have been sleeping outside in the cold, damp, dreary Ulster winter.

After a few weeks in the sometimes quiet and sometimes chaotic streets of Londonderry, we would rotate to McGilligan Camp for rest and recuperation, as the brass liked to call our visits there.

A holiday camp, it was not. It was an abandoned World War Two concentration camp that was home to countless German POWs during the war.

It wasn't exactly Colditz, but then it didn't have to be. Anyone unlucky enough to succeed in an escape attempt found themselves in boggy marshland, surrounded on three sides by the cold Irish Sea, in the middle of a cold damp Ulster winter. They're foremost thoughts must have been more of survival than that of escape.

Surrounded by high, barbed-wire fences, with watchtowers every 100 yards and enough barbed wire to keep the most determined prisoner in, and luckily for us, The Black Balaclava Boys out.

They never, for a long time, worked up enough balls to hit us at The Rest or McGilligan, and considering the amount of firepower we kept behind the barbed wire of the old prison camp and The Rest, that was no wonder.

Their forte was roadside bombs, or snipers, or rioting in the streets. The Americans were supplying them with money and a trickle of arms, all unofficially, of course. But then a North African donut, with money coming out of his ears, decided to dip his toes in the water and he decided to provide The Black Balaclava Boys with a shipload of ordinance.

This, unfortunately, went to their heads and suddenly they thought they could match our firepower. As it turned out, a big mistake on the part of their Army Council.

They would meet the freighters out in the Irish Sea and offload their cargo to fishing boats and then transport the arms and explosives to the mainland, where it was loaded onto lorries. Then it would disappear into the countryside to concealed arms cashes.

With these shipments coming in regularly, their stores of modern weapons were built up and with them their confidence finally got so high that they decided to take the tiger by the tail and got the balls to take us on in our barbed-wire holiday camp at McGilligan Point.

The night they decided to come for us was a typical McGilligan Point night – cold, wet, windy and foggy. The sentries on the main gate and the watchtowers were hindered with 50-foot visibility and freezing with the brass monkeys.

I was off duty that night, curled up in my warm bed after a pint in the NAAFI, reading a good book, listening to the bad weather outside and thanking my lucky stars that I didn't have to be outside, when my nice warm night was shattered by small arms' fire and two roaring explosions at the main gate. Shit, so much for my night off.

McGilligan was so well fortified that they had to have something new up their sleeves, something outstanding to give them the guts to hit us there, head on.

They had hit the gate with HE rounds from a Carl Gustav – the modern equivalent to the old bazooka. Jesus, what else did they have?

I rolled out of my bunk and grabbed my rifle and my webbing. I had a full magazine on my SLR and six spare magazines in my webbing – enough to be going on with.

The small arms' fire was still coming in from all sides, but the explosions had come from the main gate so that was the way to go. If they managed to knock out our main gate we would really be in a world of hurt.

When I reached the gates they were on fire, the guard posts either side were burning and the sentries were down. We needed some heavy firepower here and we needed it damned fast.

The night sky was rent by flames and we were deafened by explosion after explosion. Things were looking bad at that moment.

As I approached the gates, Webber ran up and shouted, "Jesus, Mac, let's see if we can get the machine guns from the guard posts going, or we are really going to be in deep shit!"

We had tripod-mounted GPMGs on either side of the gate and if we could get them working again we could throw a devastating amount of fire down the road to our front.

I jumped down behind the sandbags and wrestled the big gun back upright and luckily it wasn't damaged and still had a belt in it.

As I opened with the heavy 7.62 GPMG, the Black Balaclava Boys scrambled to get out of the way, some of them weren't fast enough and they were shredded where they stood by the heavy bullets.

Just then Webber jumped down into the pit beside me carrying more boxes of ammunition for the heavy gun.

"Keep them away from the gate, Mac, while I go and organise the rest of the boys!"

Just then one of the new boys ran past, a young private; I still didn't know his name. The big guy grabbed him and dragged him into the hole with us.

Webber told him to stay with me as the number two on the gun. We had to keep laying down fire to our front to keep them away from the gate, and at the rate I was throwing it down that road we were lucky to have the two spare barrels for the gun there because the barrel was beginning to turn red.

We had big problems with these guns when they were first issued and they took away our trusty Bren Guns. The original barrels for the GPMG had a nickeloid lining that would hold its original size as the gun heated up, and the result was an overheated barrel that was expanding while the lining stayed the same size and eventually dropped out. Which was no fun in a firefight like this. But, happily, this problem was sorted or we would be in deep shit.

Anyway, we carried on laying a heavy rate of fire keeping The Black Balaclava Boys at bay, and it was absolute chaos with small arms' fire rattling continuously. Rocket propelled grenades were hitting our towers; you could tell the boys had been receiving heavy shipments of arms by the way they were expending huge amounts of ordinance.

This was turning out to be worse than any bad Saturday night in the streets. The gatehouse was on fire and the ground was littered with bodies; luckily most of them were dressed in black. This was turning into a real charnel house. My next burst from the heavy gun shredded a screaming soldier of the revolution and he went down in a heap with his blood spraying everywhere.

These guys must have been high on drugs, probably PCPs, because they just kept coming, even with enough lead in them to put them on their arse long before.

Shit, this was definitely not normal; that bloody freighter must have been carrying a lot more than arms. One guy went down with his chest a bloody mess from the big machine gun, normally enough to finish the biggest man, but his fingers kept squeezing the trigger of his AK47.

I didn't know how much longer we could keep them out of the wire at this rate. Shit, where was our quick reaction force? They should have been with us by now. We kept a helicopter borne quick reaction force at Belfast on duty 24 hours a day, just for such an emergency. The fact that we hadn't seen them yet made me think that the radio shack had been the first to get hit. If so, we were in even more shit.

With tracer rounds splitting the night and the crackle of small arms' fire and explosions everywhere, things were rapidly going from bad to worse. I spotted a screaming nutter making for the guardhouse and I let go of the GPMG long enough to give him a double tap from my SLR and he went down like a sack of shit. I didn't want to fire the machine at the guardhouse in case we still had anyone alive in there.

We had gone too far to worry about shooting a man in the back; this was turning into a kill-or-be-killed madhouse now. When I picked up the GPMG again I burnt my hand on the barrel so it was time for another barrel change and then I could start laying fire down on the road to my front.

I hoped that Webber was getting the perimeter guardpost organised because I could only concentrate on what was to my front. The new boy did his job and kept feeding me belt after belt for the machine gun. Between us we were turning the area in front of the main gates into a veritable butcher shop; the lad was certainly in for some bad nightmares in the near future.

Suddenly a body slammed into the gun-pit beside me, startling me so much that I nearly left him with a bayonet in the throat, as an automatic reaction, out of pure abject fear.

Webber laughed like a drain, as he stuck an arm like a small tree over my hand holding the bayonet.

"Shit, Mac, I'm on your side!" and he roared with laughter. All this shit coming down on our heads and the big fart could still make a joke about it.

He was carrying two more boxes of ammunition for the machine gun and he shouted above the bedlam, "Come on, Mac. If these assholes want to take our barbed-wire holiday camp, let's make them pay dearly for it!"

I looked at the big fart's grinning face beside me and I thought, bugger it, if they were going to take this place from us then we would have to make it very, very expensive for them.

Webber had an SLR with him and he took great delight in adding to the bedlam by expending magazine after magazine to our front, while I carried on with the ever-hotter GPMG, sending burst after burst of devastating fire into the vehicles to our front trying to get to our more and more bedraggled main gate.

The GPMGs in the towers were pouring concentrated fire into the nutters in front of us, when some of our boys turned up with a Carl Gustav, the modern equivalent of the old-fashioned bazooka, and started whacking round after round into the vehicles in front of us.

The night was rent by fire and explosives as we continued to fight for our lives, but I think that was when the tide started to turn and the screwballs in front of us were finding out that they had bitten off more than they could chew.

Webber was happily whacking out magazine after magazine from his SLR and my machine gun barrel was getting hotter and hotter. It was nearly time for another barrel change because with the amount of lead I was sending their way, my gun was getting bloody hot.

But we were finally pushing them back with the help of the Carl Gustav crew and the gun crew on the other side of the gate. They started to fall back and we moved forward, pressing them all the time.

I still couldn't understand why they had taken us on at McGilligan in the first place, even with the extra supplies coming from the freighter off the coast; it just wasn't like them to go up against odds like this.

Then as we moved forward onto the road in front of the camp, I finally got my answer. I knelt down and pulled the balaclava from a dying, bloodied man and got the shock of my life. He wasn't Irish at all, he was North African, and drugged up to the eyeballs. They were using mercenaries.

No wonder it had taken so much to push them back. He was up to his eyeballs with PCPs and feeling no pain at all; a condition that these soldiers of Allah liked to fight their battles in.

"Have a look here, sir," I called to Webber.

"Shit, bloody mercenaries," he growled. "No wonder they gave us so much trouble."

They were pulling out but definitely not finished yet.

Webber shouted, "Get your wagon, Mac, and I'll organise some more bodies. We're not finished with these nutters yet."

Tired bloody and dirty as we were, we soon got my wagon, followed by two three-tonners, each carrying a fully armed platoon. We were chasing the bastards back to the coast and every man with us wanted blood after what these nutters had put us through.

They didn't try to lay any traps for us; they just ran for the coast, their ship and escape, they hoped. We were running straight at them, carrying enough firepower to put them on the bottom of the Irish Sea.

When we hit the coast, we could see four Zodiac rubber boats heading out to the freighter that was lying off the coast, obviously waiting for what was left of their attacking force.

We had four GPMGs with us, which we promptly set up and once again tracer rounds lit up the night as we started to lay down fire on the vulnerable rubber boats.

Then it was the turn of the Carl Gustav crew to happily bang away with high-explosive rounds on them and the freighter, which was nearly at the limit of their range. Even so, they were soon scoring hits, which must have pissed off the captain no end.

Just then, a Land Rover and trailer pulled up with a squeal of brakes. Sergeant Danny Lane was on board with an 81mm mortar crew. He jumped out with an ear to ear grin and shouted to Webber, "Is this a private party, sir, or can anyone join in?"

"Get set up quick, Danny!" roared the big guy. "The more the merrier at this party."

And soon we had the "poom, poom, poom" of the mortar, the chatter of the guns and the roar of the HE rounds. With the tracer rounds lighting up the sky, the mercenaries of Allah were soon between a rock and a very hard place and I didn't think they would be having a go at our holiday camp again any time soon.

The Zodiacs were being shredded by the GPMGs and the mortar and the Carl Gustav were scoring regular hits on the rust bucket of a freighter. The captain of the ship finally realised he was in a bad place and decided that discretion really was the better part of valour; he was getting under way, turning out to sea and leaving his merry band of warriors to the cold waters.

But he wasn't out of danger yet, as our mortar and Carl Gustav were still pouring round after round into his small rusty vessel. There were fires on deck and it looked in a seriously bad way as he finally pulled out of our range.

"Cease fire! Cease fire!" shouted Webber. "Leave some for the Royal Navy boys to clear up."

What a wind down; they had put holes in our defences around McGilligan, but in the end we sent the swarthy mercenaries on their way and the little colonel's attempt at a

Navy was limping out into the cold waters of the Irish Sea, licking their wounds and trying unsuccessfully to outrun the Senior Service boys.

We had also decimated their soldiers for hire, who would probably never want to get mixed up with the Provo's again. Now it was back to McGilligan to clean up the mess.

When we got back there was a smouldering mess waiting for us. The boys had already started the clean-up and were sorting out the butcher's bill.

Parker met us at what was left of the main gate of our barbed-wire holiday camp.

The quick reaction force were finally there and had already started to evacuate the casualties, who would go first to the Royal Belfast Hospital to stabilize them for the onward journey to England and eventually the Selly Oak Hospital in Birmingham.

Parker told us that the final count for us was two dead, who would make the final journey home in a body bag. There were also six severely wounded, who would probably recover but never see active service again, and ten with minor wounds who would recover and probably be back with us after a few months' treatment.

As for the mercenaries that had the hard neck to take us on at McGilligan, well, they weren't anywhere near as lucky, that's if you could call what we had been through lucky. So far the count was 20 dead and rising, with six more so severely wounded that they had virtually no chance of recovery. But these six and the rest with minor wounds were being treated by our medics with a view to the survivors ending up in an English prison.

All in all, a costly excursion for the Provo's and their Mercs. They had taken a big hit that night and I thought it would be a long time before they worked up enough courage to try us on our home ground again.

We were bloodied but not beaten. We had casualties, of course, we had two men in body bags and several of our boys would be keeping the excellent medics back at Selly Oak busy for a few months, but they were already looking forward to the company of some nice nurses. But we would rebuild our barbed-wire holiday camp, and it would take time, but morale would soon be as high as it was before that night. The engineers were already hard at work rebuilding the headquarters' office and re-establishing communications, which had been cut in the battle and was the number one priority job.

Just then Webber wandered out of the turmoil in the headquarters' building and his rumbling laugh could be heard 20 yards away.

I said, "What are you so happy about, sir?"

He chuckled, "One of the chopper jockeys just picked up a radio message. It seems the Senior Service boys intercepted our rust-bucket freighter and he wouldn't heave-to when told to and he wouldn't answer any radio messages, so the brass authorised them to sink him, which they promptly did! This little outing just gets more and more expensive for the bad guys!" And he walked off, just chortling away.

And after all we had been through, tired and battered as we were, once again the big guy could bring a smile to our faces.

Chapter Six

Observation Post

When 14 Company came up with intelligence on an arms cache, usually out in the boonies somewhere on a remote farm, it was up to us to mount an observation post to check it out; we were "on observation" in army parlance.

Now this wasn't just turning up to watch the place, which was what we had to do, but it was far more complicated than that. We had to go in unseen at night, a severe test of our woodcraft skills, and be prepared for long periods, keeping tabs on the place. We had to take everything in with us: arms, ammunition, food and water, bottled water, Mars Bars (which were a firm favourite) and also day- and night-vision gear. And we could leave nothing behind when we left.

When I say we could leave nothing behind, that means absolutely nothing. If you needed a slash, it was into an empty water bottle, if you needed a crap, it was into a plastic zip-lock bag, and it all had to come with us when we left the site, crap and all, and this was where you found out who your real friends were, after all, someone had to hold the bag for you while you had a crap.

But along with all these fun and games, there was a very serious side. If your field-craft wasn't up to scratch and the boys discovered your position, you would have to shoot your way out; there was no way they were going to get help to you in time to avoid it. And two men shooting their way out of a mess like that when we didn't know what we were going to face, you have to remember there was definitely no shortage of guns in the Province, then or now, so the last thing we wanted was a shoot-out; in and out unobserved was the way to go.

The call came down from 14 Company on a cold dreary Friday; they had the skinny on a suspected arms cache near Coleraine, on a remote farm. Now like I said before, this was a severe test of our woodcraft skills.

We had to slip in under cover of darkness to an LUP, a lying up position, invisible to anyone on the farm, bringing in enough supplies for up to a week, including ammunition and night and day observation gear, and be able to get out again taking absolutely everything with us and leaving no sign that you had ever been there.

Now let these bankers and city workers tell you that they have the most stressful job on the planet. Yeah, right. Substitute the "b" for a "w" and you're getting somewhere near the truth; what a load of wimps.

At the briefing, Webber decided that I was just the bloke to go on this little jaunt with a newly arrived corporal named Jerry Blane, a first-timer in the Province and fresh from corporal's course, which he unfortunately thought covered for any lack of experience on his part. Oh, what fun and games we had in front of us.

"Come on, Mac, you old bugger, he has to get experience somehow. Why not with you?" And Webber walked away from me chuckling to himself while the air around me was turning blue as I was coming up with swear words that even Webber had not heard before.

And he laughed even louder when he heard me trying to explain to the very green and cabbage-like corporal why we needed a good supply of plastic bags.

We had got all the intelligence from the longhair from 14 Company, including the layout of the place and which bush was to be our home for the next few days and nights. Now it was time to go and collect supplies and ammunition.

As I went to draw ammunition for my SLR, Webber said, "Leave that, Mac, we want you to take the sniper rifle." Jesus, I thought, this day just gets better and better.

Webber saw the look on my face and he turned to the guy from 14 Company and said, "Go on, tell him the rest."

The longhair said, "This is fresh intelligence just come in. We've been told that Eddie Keogh will be there."

Keogh was a high-ranking IRA hit man who had been on the top of our wanted list for months. We knew he had just got back from America where he had been raising money for arms and it was said that he was responsible for the deaths of at least three soldiers.

"Jesus, sir," I swore at Webber, something that was not wise at the best of times but I didn't care, this was too much. "The choice of weapon tells me that you want me to slot this bastard if he comes to the farm, and you want me to do it from an isolated observation post, with a green corporal in tow."

I had just upset my observation buddy for the next few days, something that was unwise at the best of times, let alone with what we had to face over the next few days, but I didn't care, this was out of order.

Webber said, "Suck it up, old man, you're the only one available at short notice that has sniper training, and Blane isn't here for an easy ride. He needs to gain experience and to do it fast."

I said, "What about exfil? As I slot him the place will turn into a hornet's nest."

"Yeah, we've thought of that, Mac. As soon as you spot him, give us a buzz on the radio and we'll get the quick reaction force in the air and then when you confirm kill we'll move in and take out the farm and everyone on it, and that way if anyone slips past the roadblocks at least we will get Keogh."

"Jesus, sir, that's got more holes in it than a sieve, and you know it."

"I know, Mac," he said, "but we don't have time to organise anything else."

Just then Blane piped up to voice his complaints and the big guy rounded on him. "If you keep your mouth shut and listen to everything this old bugger tells you, you might, just might, come back from this in one piece."

"Yes, sir," said a very unhappy, green corporal.

Anyway, we got everything loaded on a Land Rover and headed for our drop-off point, about two miles from the farm. From there we had to move into our designated LUP and get our observation point all sorted out before daylight.

At daybreak we were settled into our cosy little nest and the new boy was still unhappy about the way things were going on his tour of the Province. But I had too many other things on my mind to be worried about him chucking his toys out of the pram – things like surviving this little jaunt – because if the boys ever discovered our lair, the results would be very messy.

We were all set up with eyes on the front of the run-down old farmhouse and outbuildings, when the new boy started whinging about needing a crap. Jesus, we were only about four and a half hours into a set up that could last for days and he was already at it.

He started to crawl back out of our hidey hole and I said, "Jesus Christ, just what the hell do you think you're doing?"

He said, "I had a curry last night and it's just beginning to work on me."

I pulled my bayonet out and slammed it into the ground in front of him. I said, "If you move one inch outside our bivvie, I will be working on you. Use the goddamn plastic bags that you brought with you."

Then the air in our little hideout proceeded to turn green, it was worse than a CS gas attack.

Finally he got himself sorted out and then we got on with the job that we had come for. We sorted out weapons and ammunition and I set up the long gun and zeroed in on the front door of the farmhouse. The rangefinder told me it was just over 900 metres, just a walk in the park for the gear that I had brought in. Well, it would be if Keogh ever showed up. One shot, one kill, just like the text books. I was confident of that. I was also sure that my biggest problem over the next few days would be the soft lad next to me. As I said before, a soldier's life on active service is long, long bouts of complete boredom followed by short periods of blinding adrenalin filled sheer terror and we were now into the long boring bit.

There was suddenly movement at the front door as a boy armed with an AK47 came out and did a circuit of the farm, checking everything out. We were obviously in the right place; he was the sentry, the dikker. Blane whispered into the radio telling Webber and the boys back at the base of the movement and that we were okay. Apart from the boy doing his patrol every couple of hours, that was it. A long boring day in front of us, leading to a long boring night when we switched over to the eerie, cold green light of the headache-inducing night observation gear and more boredom, so I told the new boy to get in some kip; we would take it in turns for some sack time.

And so it dragged on, the same routine with just the boy with AK wandering around every couple of hours. It was pure boredom but also an underlying building tension. My young partner was wilting so I hoped something would happen soon. No wonder the British Army has a drink problem and a high occurrence of ulcers, the tension was getting unbearable. But the drink problem was infinitely preferable to the American boys' problems with hard drugs in the jungle hell-holes of Vietnam.

Finally, on the third day at about 1000 hours, we finally had a break. A battered old Mazda pulled up in front of the farmhouse and three guys got out. Two I didn't recognise but the third had curly brown hair and the hard flat-eyed features of a reptile. It was Eddie Keogh and the man would take great delight in taking us apart piece by piece if we were ever discovered.

I nodded to the boy, we were on, and he sent a whispered radio message back to HQ and the hunt was on. I certainly hoped that Webber had the QRF boys in the air and the roadblocks going in. I didn't know how much help I was going to get from the soft lad if it came down to a fire-fight.

Keogh and his friends went into the farmhouse and they stayed there for about five minutes. When they came out they went across to the barn and went inside. I began to flex my muscles to loosen up my joints from the long enforced stillness in our hide. I glanced at my young partner and whispered, "We're on." He just looked sick.

I readied the long gun, slowly moving the safety catch to fire, and began to slow my breathing down. We were coming up to the short, sharp period of blinding action and I hoped that my young friend wouldn't freeze up on me as there was no room for passengers in the next few minutes.

Keogh and his mates came out of the barn and loaded some bundles into the boot of the Mazda. All my concentration was on the hit man, the other guys were on the edge of vision and there was only me and Keogh.

Suddenly I heard the "whup, whup, whup" of the choppers coming in, right on time. Keogh looked up to the sky in alarm as I took a deep breath and let half of it out then held it. Keogh was frozen there for a split second and then there was a crack from my long gun as it slammed back into my shoulder. My bullet took him high in the chest as he was lifted off his feet and thrown backwards. A small entrance hole appeared in the front of his chest and there was a red spray of blood, bone and flesh from his back. I didn't need a second look to know that he was finished. I gave my young friend a kick to get him moving. Our bit was done, the rest was up to the quick reaction force and the roadblocks.

We grabbed all of our gear, shit bags and all, crawled out of our hide and legged it for our extraction point 500 yards to the rear. No need for a quiet woodcraft withdrawal, the place was in an uproar now.

We headed for the big Wessex helicopter coming in to land and I pushed the boy on board, hastily followed by all our gear, then we were thankfully airborne.

The loadie chucked me a pair of earphones and plugged them in and then I was talking to Parker back at McGilligan on a secure net.

"They're all in the bag back at the farm. Target is down and they're clearing up the arms cache. Are you two all right? How did the new boy do?"

I said, "Yeah, we're all right, sir. We'll see you soon." I didn't tell him the soft lad was in the corner chucking up and the loadie was grumbling about clearing up the mess.

When we got back to camp, we had time to clean weapons, although the boy hadn't fired a shot, before we went for the debrief when Webber got back.

"Good job, Mac," he said. "We got all the arms, four IRA men are headed for the Maze and the families of the soldiers that bastard Keogh killed have reason to thank you, if only we could tell them what happened. That was a good shot, you old bugger."

"Not that good, sir," I said. "I was aiming for centre mass and I hit him high in the chest."

Webber laughed and said, "You fussy old bugger," and my young green friend turned an even deeper shade of green.

Chapter Seven

Snatch Squad

It was another bad Saturday night in Derry, the boys were out in force, and we were stretched to the limit all over the old city. We already had two men in hospital with bullet wounds and one with third-degree burns from petrol bombs. The crackle of small arms' fire could be heard all over the town and there were several fires burning in the Bogside and it was still only 2000 hours and we were already pushed to the limit; it was going to be a bloody night.

Webber was his usual noisy self when he went through The Sailor's Rest, rousting everyone out.

"Come on, you lazy bastards, draw ammo from the stores and get yourselves out by the wagons in full kit in ten minutes. This is shaping up to be our worst night yet."

I could see he was a worried man and that was not like him at all.

When we formed up in the car park Major Parker came out to give us the good news.

"Right, lads. We've got intel coming in from all directions. This is going to be a night of concentrated terrorist activity all over the city," he said, "and I want Number One Platoon in the market square covering the entrance to William Street." My favourite place, I don't think, and he carried on. "And I want Number Two Platoon up at Rosemount to reinforce the Redcaps there and get

Number Three Platoon up on the Derry Wall so we can have some sort of control over the high ground."

So off we jolly well went for a night of fun and games. I was with Number One Platoon manning the barricades, where William Street came into the market square, and as usual, this was the hot spot.

Major Parker shouted to Webber, "Let's get the snatch squad organised so we can thin out these crowds a bit."

Things were getting a bit busy in William Street.

Now the snatch squad was made up from ten of the biggest men we had on duty at the time, armed with hickory riot batons, no rifles and wearing facemasks, flak vests and heavy gloves. The idea was for the squad to hide behind the building where the barricades butted up to it. Then someone had to parade up and down in front of the crowd taunting them.

Of course, the man for this job had to be Webber, he loved to taunt the crowd till they were so wound up they would make a mad rush for him. Then he would stand there waiting for them till they got close enough, then the barricades would crash back and the boys would rush out and collar as many rioters as they could.

If you can picture the most violent, dirty bar fight that you can imagine and then multiply that by ten, you will get somewhere near the complete and utter violence of this exercise. Broken bones were common on both sides; my nose was broken twice doing this, and sometimes the injuries were much worse than mere broken bones. It was incredibly dangerous to run out into a crowd, armed with only a riot baton in your hand, without your rifle or sidearm, in a town where every bugger and his mum are armed and they could open fire at any time.

Anyway, the idea was for the snatch squad to do just that, to snatch them and bundle them in behind the barricades where they were arrested and marched off to the local lock-up, arriving there completely bruised and battered.

41

Some reporters then turned up with photographers to record what was happening, or so they said, and this was the last thing we needed, a bunch of pen-pushers getting in our way. One photographer had the bright idea to set off his powerful flash gun in our eyes every time we made a rush out to grab some more prisoners. Time and time again he was told not to do it; to run out into the crowd with our eyes dazzled by the flash just as a shower of bricks and assorted missiles was coming our way was extremely dangerous, but that was just what the photographer wanted.

Well, after a while we were so fed up with this idiot that I gave Alfie McGuire the wink and told him to follow my lead this time and he nodded with a big grin on his face. Alfie and I made sure we didn't have a prisoner on the way back in, so as we went past this idiot, the boys saw what we were doing and crowded around to cover us from the officers. Alfie slipped his skid lid off as we went past and cracked him over the head with it hard enough to give him a concussion and the boys were crowded around as I took his expensive flash gun and threw it into a trash can. Then we arrested him and dragged him off to the lock-up with copious amounts of blood running down his face and the beginnings of a raging headache. When the complaints came back from his newspaper the following week, there were innocent soldiers all over the place; as far as we were concerned he was just another rioter. But not surprisingly, we never had that problem again with reporters.

Well, that got the reporters out of our hair and as it turned out they didn't realise just how lucky they were as the night had much more in store for us. Webber continued to do his thing and upset as many locals as he could in one night.

The snatch squad carried on doing their thing and the local nick was starting to fill up. Then the local boys decided to wind the proceedings up a notch. My co-conspirator with the photographer and his flash gun suddenly decided to put a nifty turn of speed on our next charge into the crowd. As we closed in with the crowd, Alfie was about ten feet in front of the pack, not a good place to be under those circumstances as it only draws attention to you at a very dangerous time, and this is what happened to Alfie.

A guy near the back of the crowd suddenly dashed to the front and threw a petrol bomb and Alfie out in front was the obvious target. Suddenly Alfie was down and engulfed in flames. Now we had a problem; we had to get the crowd far enough back so that we could get the flames out and the doc in to see to Alfie, and we had to do it damned quickly.

Webber was thinking on his feet, as usual. He had the barricades whipped back out of the way and the whole platoon rushed forward to chase the locals back out of the way. The ambulance screamed out and pulled up in front of Alfie to cover him. Then two medics jumped out on the doc's instructions, smothered the flames on Alfie and got him onto a stretcher and into the back of the ambulance. There was no time to mess about on the ground with first aid, they had to get him away and to the hospital as quickly as possible.

Now Webber was pissed off, and that was definitely a bad thing for the rioters. He got us formed up across the road and three men in the line had what we called boomers, a weapon that looked very much like a sawn-off shotgun and could be just as devastating in the right hands.

Rubber bullets were highly disliked by the locals, who had experience with these deadly weapons, and with good reason. Don't let the name rubber bullet fool you; these baton rounds were deadly when they were bounced off the road in front of the crowd of rioters.

A total of six baton rounds were fired and the effect was devastating. This effectively knocked the stuffing out of the most dedicated rioter.

Then Webber had us advance quickly up the road, weapons at the high port showing enough firepower to cause a massacre if things got out of hand.

But Webber had things under control and the crowd, showing a bit of self-control for a change, quickly dispersed. Not even a donut in a second-storey window having a few potshots at us could get things out of hand. Someone pumped a few rounds through the window he was firing from and he either died very quickly or he decided it was time for him to be elsewhere.

A good result at the end of the night but a costly one; over the whole city we had three men in hospital with serious but not terminal bullet wounds, and two men in with third-degree burns from petrol bombs. The burns victims were by far the worst off; Alfie had earned his membership to the Guinea Pig Club in East Grinstead.

We made 15 arrests that night and three of those were hospitalised with broken bones before ending up in the Maze Prison in Belfast.

All in all, just another bad night in Derry. We had seen worse.

Chapter Eight

The .38 Calibre Smith and Wesson

We had come to the end of another stint in the streets and it was time to pull back to our five-star holiday camp at McGilligan Point.

I was driving the lead Land Rover, as usual, and I had a young 19-year-old sub-lieutenant in front by the name of Kersey. He came to Northern Ireland on a commission purchased by his rich daddy. Not a good combination in the mean streets of Northern Ireland. He had a .38 Smith and Wesson, also purchased by Daddy, and he used to walk around the streets with that damned gun in his pocket and a John Wayne complex in his head. We had to look after him, as if we didn't have enough to do.

In the back of the Land Rover I had Jerry Smith, the young lieutenant's bat-man, and one other guy riding shotgun. We had a three-tonner following us with a full platoon on board and another Land Rover bringing up the rear. Tail-end Charlie was not a very good job around there, but then someone had to do it. All in all we were carrying enough firepower to keep most sensible people away, but this was Northern Ireland after all.

Now, we had been on to the brass for ages to use helicopters to move us quickly around the Province but the

MOD kept saying it was too expensive. This was politicians getting their priorities right, but believe me their priorities were not always right.

So our little convoy moved out of the city on our way to McGilligan Point and we were moving at high speed to try and put the boys off having a pop at us as we went past at a high rate of knots. We had been on the road about 20 minutes when I heard a whoosh and a boom behind us. At least one of the boys was on the ball. It was an RPG and it took out our last Land Rover as we sped past. Luckily, it struck the engine compartment and the boys on board were alive but cut and bruised and very shaken, but they came out alive.

The call came over the radio, "Tail-end Charlie is hit. His wagon is scrap and we need to stop for survivors."

I had already stopped and I baled out and took up a position covering the right flank, hoping someone was covering the left as, of course, they were. We had been doing this too long now to screw it up when it got hot. In the rear they cleared out the dead Land Rover and then we heard the radio message we were waiting for, "The Land Rover is cleared. All personnel are aboard the three-tonner. Let's get the hell out of here."

So we were off, with one less Land Rover, which was luckily the only casualty. Sometimes it was like that and this time our luck was in.

The boss got on the radio, "Put your foot down, Mac, in case there are any more of those crazy bastards around here," and I was only too happy to oblige.

We made record time back to the lovely McGilligan Camp and when we pulled up at company HQ, Lieutenant Kersey was off to do whatever it is that junior officers do and left everything in the wagon for Smith, his batman, to clear out.

As we were unloading I spotted his .38 left in the dash.

"Here, Jerry, get rid of this before young Mr Silly Bollocks drops me right in it."

Now on paper army law says that the driver of the vehicle is responsible for every weapon that comes on board being unloaded and made safe. But when the weapon in question is brought on board by an officer, junior or otherwise, that law kind of goes out the window. Smith took the boy's six-gun and all his other gear inside and I thought no more of it.

I was clearing my gear out and preparing to gas up my wagon and move it to the car park when I heard a muffled crack coming from the company office. We all knew what it was; there was no mistaking it for a car backfiring, given our location.

The next thing I knew the doc arrived at a full gallop, going straight into the office. An ice-cold feeling ran up my spine; there was only one answer, every soldier's nightmare – an accidental discharge in the company office. What have you done, Smith, you crazy bastard? And before I could get to the office, the door crashed open and Smith was doubled out under guard, heading for the lock-up.

I rushed into the office to see what had happened and found Danny Jared, with the doc frantically working on a bullet hole in his throat.

"Oh God, what has that silly bastard done?" I shouted.

Kersey was there, white-faced and shaking, and Shelley shouted at me, "Did you give that silly bugger that gun, Mac?"

But Kersey answered for me, "No, sergeant, you can't blame Mallory. I left the gun in the Land Rover. I should have picked it up."

Apparently Smith had walked into the office playing with the pistol like some demented cowboy and promptly shot Danny Jarad in the throat. And there was me saying we were professional soldiers.

Jared was lucky, he survived back in Blighty in hospital, albeit with a very squeaky voice. Smith was bundled off to Colchester to the hardest military prison in the country and I was left kicking myself for not unloading the gun before I gave it to him. We were under enough pressure on this job without having to put up with blue on blue as well.

Chapter Nine

The Bitch from the Bogside

Around about the time that Dana won the Eurovision Song Contest, we had a visit from another famous Bogside resident, the Member of Parliament for the Bogside. Bonnie Delaney decided to come home for a visit and the feedback that we were getting from 14 Company wasn't good; there were whispers on the streets that the UDR were taking an interest in her visit.

As she was Bogside Catholic through and through, the Protestants would like nothing better than have one of their own in the job, and they weren't too fussy how they went about creating a vacancy.

We had the same situation as when Dana came home from Eurovision, only this time we were looking for UDR shooters just to complicate matters, as well as doing our usual crowd control, which was more than enough to make for a very busy night.

We all knew that this job could turn into our worst nightmare in the blink of an eye. Any shooter who wasn't worried about getting away is near enough impossible to stop and to lose a Member of Parliament on our patch was unthinkable, even one as smelly as this one, and would do the reputation of the regiment no good at all.

Certainly none of us was interested in taking a bullet meant for "The Lady" although, unfortunately, that was exactly what happened, and this, by the way, was definitely no "lady". We all hoped that this routine job would not turn out to be a trip home in a body bag.

Parker had the whole company involved in this job. Number One Platoon was to cover the station when she arrived, with Two and Three covering her route at strategic points.

"The Lady", and that word was definitely used loosely, came out of the station with her people in tow, and it was easy to separate her party people from her so-called close protection. They stood out from the crowd, giving new meaning to the words "like a sore thumb", and they shouldn't have, they should have been anonymous, not standing out like the soldiers lining the route. We were dealing with amateurs and they were going to get in our way; this had the makings of a bad day already.

Webber walked down our ranks, doing his usual job of keeping us on our toes. As he passed by he growled in my ear, "Are you up for this, Mac?"

I said, "Come on, sir, you've seen the amateurs that are going to get in our way and make an impossible job even harder. You know the score."

"I know, Mac," he replied. "But as usual it's up to us to make the best of a bad job."

"Yeah," I said, "just as long as doing the job and looking after the amateurs doesn't mean more body bags."

"I couldn't agree with you more, you old bastard," he said. "But be careful out there today, it wouldn't be the same around here without your ugly mug."

"Thanks a lot," I said, "I think."

We were all fired up and on our toes; this was what the lads called "The Buzz". An adrenalin high that was addictive. "The Buzz" kept you sharp and on top of things and with what we had facing us, we needed to be sharp.

They say the British Army had a drink problem, but this was just our way of coming down from the high, when it was time to leave the streets, relax and unwind.

"The Lady" and her party exited the station and got into their cars and as they did so, we had eyes all around with special attention being paid to the surrounding rooftops. Things were going all right. So far so good, famous last words.

The convoy, with our boys in front and back, moved slowly away from the station. The route chosen was one I never would have approved of, but then, I wasn't in charge. We moved slowly through the town square and up into William Street. Really not the way to go after all the trouble we had in that area, this was definitely Indian country.

We picked our way along William Street gingerly, not knowing what to expect. Webber had half the platoon out in front running interference, two wagons on each flank and my wagon bringing up the rear as Tail-end Charlie. I had two riflemen in the back and a young corporal by the name of Simmons up in front with me.

Like I said, William Street was not my choice of route. We had already had so much trouble there and it was marked in red on the map in the headquarters situation room. As our little convoy progressed up the road, hoping against hope that things weren't about to go loud, but that was too much to ask, we were walking on eggs by this time. In fact, there was every chance that things would kick off on this one and I would have been the most surprised one there if they didn't. But then I was just a pessimistic old Yank, as the boys were fond of telling me.

As we picked our way cautiously along the road, there was suddenly a loud explosion in front of us and our convoy ground to a halt. Things had definitely gone noisy. I could see flames and smoke up in front but in the chaos I couldn't see which vehicle it was coming from.

I said, "Stand by, boys. Lock and load, things are about to get interesting."

Just then Webber came on the air, "Look alive, all call signs," he growled. "We've just tripped a roadside bomb and the car in front of Bogside One is out of action."

Bogside One was the call sign for the bitch from the Bogside and things were definitely warming up.

Then the big guy was back on the radio, "We can't move and we're expecting shooters on the rooftops," he said and his voice was showing about as much emotion as someone reading the weather report on the telly. Then he came back on the air with a laconic, "Seattle One, are you in a position to extract 'The Lady'?"

Shit, that was me! "Hang on, guys, we are just going to pick up a passenger."

Then I swung out of line and put the pedal to the metal. The sound of buzzing hornets increased as my wagon started to take on several holes from the 7.62 shorts coming from the AK47s on the rooftops.

I had my hands full weaving in and out of the stranded motors in the road while at the same time trying to keep an eye on the rooftops. I said to the young corporal next to me.

"Give the big guy a buzz on the radio and tell him we'll have a go at picking her up."

While Corporal Simmons was shouting down the radio to Webber, l shouted to the boys in the back.

"Stand by, we're going in hot to pick up 'The Lady'. And if she gives you any lip, MP or no MP, knock her out and throw her in the back of the wagon."

With the engine screaming and the crackle of small arms' fire all around us, I only had time to slam the wagon to a halt beside her car, and the boys jumped out and dragged a screaming Member of Parliament out of her car and threw her in the back of my Land Rover.

Luckily, her boys were enough on the ball to see that the best course of action was for us to get her the hell out of there as quickly as possible and they didn't interfere.

With bullets whacking into the side of my Land Rover, we had no time for finesse. I screamed at the young two-striper beside me, "Help them get her in the back or we are going to be spending more time around here than is good for our health."

It was getting hotter by the moment, with petrol bombs going off, high velocity rounds zipping past us and high explosives ripping up and down the street.

"Come on, you guys!" I shouted. "Where's our passenger?"

Just then a bloodied and bedraggled MP was bundled into the back of my wagon, screaming her head off.

I said, "For Christ's sake, shut her up, guys," as I spun the wagon around, leaving green paint on a wall and one of the cars in the convoy.

Finally I got the green machine turned around and headed off in the direction of The Sailor's Rest. She was still screaming her head off in the back, and even after all this time the overriding memory is one absolute chaos – bullets flying, bombs going off, and above all, her serious BO problem. Maybe there was a shortage of soap in the Bogside. It certainly wasn't us as we had all been down to HMS Belfast the day before for a shower.

She was still screaming in the back about my boys molesting a Member of Parliament. Silly bitch, they were in the process of saving her life. Finally, I'd had enough. Here I was speeding through the streets of Derry, in a wagon that was more suited to doing a bit of cross country, and in the process of saving her stupid life.

I exploded, "Shut up, you stupid Bogside bitch! These guys just saved you from a UDR bullet in your frigging head. Now if you can only keep your mouth shut for five minutes we might even get out of this situation and save your worthless politician life!"

It was a good job I wasn't interested in promotion, because that was certainly going to come back and bite me in the ass, but it did the trick and she finally fell silent.

I said to the boy beside me, "Get on the blower to Webber and let him know that we are on the way back to The Sailor's Rest with 'The Lady' in tow."

Webber was glad to hear the message, even though he had his hands full extracting the boys from the mess in William Street.

In the meantime, I pulled my wagon up in front of The Sailor's Rest and told the boys to take her inside under guard while I went across the road to park up my bullet-riddled Land Rover. Having a look around the wagon, it certainly looked like another one for the scrapyard.

A private called Jason was on guard there and he came over with a worried look on his face. He said, "I heard it was a bad one, Mac."

"Yeah," I said, "bad and getting worse when we left. Just count the holes in my wagon."

When I got back into The Rest, the smelly one was in full flow, bending Parker's ear about me and my boys. When I walked into his office, he shook his head and said in his ever-so-posh voice, "Miss Delaney, these men saved your life tonight and even if Private Mallory is from the Colonies, the fact remains, without him and his friends you would be laying in William Street right now with several bullets in you. A fate that some of my men still may meet today, thanks to you!"

Strong stuff from the posh lad, especially as he was talking to a serving Member of Parliament. But the old boy was pissed off. I had never heard him talk to anyone like that before, but it served the purpose and once again she shut her mouth.

I said, "How are they doing, sir? Do you need us to go out again?" Being polite was easy with him, he had earned our respect the hard way, she hadn't.

He said, "No need, Mac. It looks like the sergeant major has worked his magic again. But sadly, he has lost two men to this pointless exercise. I have a chopper coming to collect her any time now."

Just then Webber arrived and I said to "The Lady", "Miss Delaney, you should realise by now why I didn't have time to be polite to you, but we lost two men today all because you wanted to wind up the local Protestants. We don't know yet how many of their boys died and if I had taken the time to be polite, who knows how many more would have died, including you."

She just shrugged her shoulders and said, "The Protestants are no loss anyway, and as for your men, that is their job, isn't it?"

Ice cold fingers went down my spine as I came out of the chair to face her. I got as far as "you cold-hearted, scheming, political bitch" before I was bundled out the office by the bear that was Sergeant Major Webber, and deposited on a chair in his office.

He growled, "Cool it, Mac. Cool it."

He just looked at me and went to the filing cabinet and pulled out a bottle of scotch that was strictly forbidden in The Rest. Then he poured out half a glass and deposited it under my nose.

"Drink it, Mac. That's an order," he rumbled.

Booze was strictly forbidden here as we were on active service after all, but I was so pissed off I grabbed the glass and downed it in one.

I looked the big guy straight in the eye and said, "Jesus, sir, it's times like this that I want to walk away from your damned army and go back to the States!"

He looked me in the eye as he refilled my glass and said, "Go back, Mac, back to the country that collects money to finance the IRA."

I poured the whisky back in the bottle and said, "No, I'll stay and finish the job, sir. But when we get back to McGilligan, the drinks are on you."

The big guy just sat there with a thoughtful look on his face. Then he said, "Yes, you old Yankee bastard, I'll buy all the drinks you want as long as you help me get these kids through this and safely back to England."

There could only be one answer to that, it had to be yes.

Chapter Ten

The Car Park

Opposite The Sailor's Rest we had a secure compound where we kept all of our vehicles. It had to be secure to keep the Balaclava Boys from paying us a visit in the night, and leaving us a surprise for the morning.

The surprise would have been a lump of plastic explosive that would have left driver and vehicle spread all over the compound, not doing the driver, or the vehicle, or our street cred any good at all. Now you probably think that the last one would not be of any importance at all, but you would be very wrong. We survived that place by having street cred, once we lost that we would be well and truly in deep shit.

One night I drew the ten-till-midnight stag as the compound sentry. It was a two-hour stag, which went by quickly with no problems. I was in contact with The Rest by radio and I had half-hourly visits from the corporal of the guard and his colleagues. I spent my two hours checking all the vehicles, paying particular attention to the rear of the compound, back by the river, and my two hours went quickly and quietly and without any problems. But I was still glad to see my relief coming out of The Rest with the corporal of the guard, Tim Dalton, who was an old hand at this silly game of soldiers and my relief was Sammy Field, a new boy fresh out from England.

"Where are you, Mac?" Tim called out quietly as they came into the car park.

I slipped out from in between two vehicles and came up behind them and said quietly, "Here I am."

They both jumped and Tim turned to me and said, "Jesus, I wish you wouldn't do that, you old Yankee bastard. Are you part Indian or something?"

I said, "Yeah, as a matter of fact I am. Sorry, guys, but on a job like this, the best place to be is in the shadows."

Sammy wasn't looking to happy; this was his first time in the car park.

I said, "You all right, Sammy? I haven't seen anyone all night. It's too cold and wet for the boys to be out tonight."

But he still didn't look too happy. I said to Tim, "You'll have to keep a close eye on our Sammy tonight, he doesn't look too good."

Tim said, "Yeah, I think you're right, Mac."

When I got back to The Rest I had a quick coffee in the canteen to warm myself up and headed for my bed for some kip.

It seemed like only minutes had gone by after I had closed my eyes, when I was rudely awakened with the place in an uproar.

I staggered from my room, rifle in hand and webbing with five extra magazines in the other hand, just in case the boys had finally gotten the balls to take us on in The Rest. But I couldn't really believe that, considering the firepower we had in there. Still, with the soldiers of the revolution, we never knew what they would get up to next.

Luckily that wasn't it, although, as things turned out, I almost wished that was the case.

As Dick Shelley came rushing past, I shouted, "What's occurring, Sarge?"

He said, "It looks like that new boy, Field, has thrown a wobbly and took a shot at Tim Dalton and the relief sentry."

"Jesus, Sarge, he didn't look too good when he came to relieve me."

Shelley said, "It looks like he's cracked up, he must have thought the IRA were after him. Anyway he shot Tim and we don't know how bad he is yet. Every time we try to get to him Sammy opens fire again."

"Bloody hell, Sarge," I said. "What happens now? I mean, if he's gone section eight and he's shooting our boys, what happens now?"

He said grimly, "If we can't talk him round and calm him down, then it's a decision for the officers. We can't let him carry on shooting our boys. I don't know what's going on in his head, Mac, but we have to sort it out before daylight."

When we got to the car park, Major Parker was there with Webber trying to make sense of a bad situation and Sammy Field was so far gone by now that he was shooting at anyone who came within range. Tim was down on his back, behind a Land Rover with the doc working on him.

Major Parker said, "How is he doing, doc?"

"He'll be all right when we can get him to hospital but it's 50-50 whether he keeps his arm!"

But we still had to get Sammy back down to earth and at this point in time no one had any idea how we were going to do that. We couldn't get his gun away from him and as the hours drew by, Sammy withdrew deeper and deeper into himself and became more and more convinced that he was shooting at IRA men, no matter what we said to him.

He was getting worse by the minute, and he still had a loaded SLR in his hands.

Webber came past and said, "Jesus, Mac, I don't know what to say or what to do now."

This was something that we had never heard from the big guy before.

I said, "Bloody hell, sir, you don't expect one of us to shoot him, do you?"

Just then there was a flurry of shots from the car park. Then after a few minutes, as we stood there wondering what was going to happen, the boys came back carrying a body. The reaction from all the guys there was one of total disbelief. Jesus, not one of our own? But it was, sadly. It was one of our own. One who could not handle the stress of the situation that we were in there. One that never should have been sent there in the first place. Someone back at headquarters in England should have spotted this when he was doing his training. The system had certainly let this kid down and Parker had to give the order to shoot him.

Now I was no stranger to shooting and I could shoot when we had to, but I could never have given that order or taken that shot. I still don't know to this day how Parker did it, or how it affected him in the years to come. Very badly I'm sure.

Chapter Eleven

The Guinness Factory

We were all lazing about The Sailor's Rest one morning when Webber's dulcet tones boomed out around the place.

"Come on, you lazy bastards. Get yourselves sorted out in full kit by the wagons in ten minutes. Riflemen with 80 rounds each, GPMG, gunners with 400 rounds. We've just had a call, the silly bastards have left a bomb in the local Guinness factory. That's a brewery to you and me."

Obviously, the first reaction was "Let the bastards blow it up, we don't want the stuff anyway, and they put it on their cornflakes. How is blowing that up going to hurt us?"

But Webber was way ahead of us.

"Never mind the bullshit, you lot. We've got to cordon the place off while the bomb disposal boys work their magic."

Of course, while I was mumbling "I hope they realise that we are being set up for an ambush", Webber, with his radar ears, picked it up.

"Shut up, Mac, you lazy old Yankee bastard. Get your gear on and get down by your wagon."

Hell, anyone would think he had a complex about Yanks. Anyway, we all piled into the wagons. I was driving Captain Teale and Webber was in the back with two riflemen. We had a three-tonner following us with a full platoon in it.

The hair was standing up on the back of my neck; this was wrong, it didn't look good. Why would they want to blow the place up? They loved Guinness.

Anyway, we pulled up outside the Guinness factory and the boys piled out, quickly forming a cordon around the place. I took my place in the line, following orders, but I didn't like it.

Webber came past, checking the line and he stopped by me.

"What's up with you, you old bugger? You look a bit green around the gills."

I said, "Come on, sir, you know me. I always do my job but this is all wrong, it's got to be an ambush."

"Oh, leave it out, you old sod," and he walked away, chuckling to himself.

Sergeant Delaney walked past, checking the line himself.

"What's up with you, Mallory?" he growled. "This is not like you."

"Well, maybe it's not, Sarge," I replied. "But this doesn't feel right. Come on, you're Irish, would you blow up the only Guinness factory in town?"

"No, I don't suppose I would," he said. "But we are here till bomb disposal do their thing, so look sharp you lot."

Well, the bomb disposal boys turned up and did their thing. After half an hour they came out with five gallons of petrol that had been wired up to five pounds of plastic explosive. This was more than enough to do the job.

The bomb disposal boys were packing their gear away and getting ready to move off when Delaney came past.

"You must be getting old, Mallory," he laughed.

I was still sweating and said, "It's not over yet, Sarge."

I said to Corporal Smith on my right and Jimmy Mason on my left, "This is all wrong, boys. Keep your eyes on the buildings across the road. We're not out of this yet."

Then it came. There was a crack and right next to me there was a sound like a hammer hitting a lump of meat and I didn't have to look at Jimmy Mason to know he had been hit. I saw a flash of movement in a third-floor window opposite us and a gun barrel was being hastily withdrawn. I dropped to one knee and put half a mag of 7.62 through the offending window. The rest of the guys saw what I was doing and followed suit.

Then Webber's dulcet tones could be heard over the crackle of small arms' fire, "Cease fire! Cease fire!"

The guys blasted the front door of the house open and moved in to clear it. After about five minutes they came back out. Two guys were dragging an obviously dead man between them and a third was carrying an AK47.

The dead man looked about 30, but it wasn't easy to tell with the amount of 7.62 that he had absorbed. Webber came past and stopped to talk to me while I was getting my wagon ready for the off.

He said, "You were right, you old git. But how did you know?"

I said, "Shit, it doesn't matter how I knew. It just didn't feel right. But the real problem is that Mason has to go back to Blighty as a cripple."

Webber said, "It could have been worse. He could have gone home in a body bag, like so many others."

I had to agree with the big man. After all, we were all trying to avoid that body bag. Some were lucky and some weren't.

Chapter Twelve

The Kettle

In the early days when we first went to Derry, it was like any other posting. When we were off duty we could don civvies and go down to the pub for a relaxing drink. At that time, the worry was that the American Army had a drug problem and the British Army had a drink problem. I think we in the British Army had it the right way around.

But things had to change drastically when two young Argyll Southerland privates were having a drink in a pub in Belfast and two young dolly birds chatted them up and asked them back to their flat for a drink. The boys naturally thought they had pulled; they were normal kids doing normal things, soldiers but still teenagers. After a couple of drinks and having a laugh, the girls excused themselves to go to the loo. Normal so far, but that was about to change. A tragedy was in the making.

The boys were sitting there chatting when the gunmen rushed in and started shooting. These boys were not killed in action as all soldiers know might happen when they are on active service, they were murdered, a cold-blooded execution. And it was a double tragedy – they were teenaged twin brothers.

After that, the orders came around that no one was to go out in civvies and any drinking was to be done back at McGilligan, our luxurious rest camp, when we rotated back to the streets for our R&R time off. What a place that was; rest camp, my ass. It was an old Second World War POW camp at McGilligan Point; a freezing cold damp shit hole on the coast near Coleraine.

Anyway, when this order came out we were billeted at the five-star Sailor's Rest, a run-down old seamen's mission, that was actually like a five-star hotel compared to our first billet, which was an old railway shed open at both ends to the elements, and the elements in Northern Ireland are seriously damp and cold in the winter. It was definitely not the place to be sleeping outside.

The highlight of our week was a visit to HMS Belfast to use their shower blocks, when we were getting a bit smelly. Nowadays she's moored at London Bridge as a tourist attraction. My memories of the Belfast are certainly not as a tourist attraction. Anyone who served in the Province would at that time only remember her as a lifesaver. There are not many good memories from that time but the Belfast has to be one of them. On the other side of the coin the list of bad memories is a long one.

Before the no civvies order came around and when we were still allowed down the pub, I was off duty one night and didn't feel like sitting around The Sailor's Rest all night listening to Kenny Rogers singing about Ruby not taking her love to town, which was top of the pops on our jukebox in The Sailor's Rest.

Why it was so popular, I really don't know. It was about a wounded GI coming home from the Vietnam war without all his working parts downstairs, after stepping on an anti-personnel mine, and leaving him incapable of satisfying his wife. Now why that would be so popular, considering where we were and what we were doing, I really don't know. But maybe that's how soldiers do what we have to do, by having a morbid sense of humour.

Anyway, that night I just didn't fancy sitting around The Sailor's Rest listening to Kenny, as much as I like country music.

Dick Shelley, the platoon sergeant, shouted out as I approached the door, "If you're going out, Mac, take this kettle up to Rosemount School for the Redcaps billeted up there on your way to the pub. That'll save us sending out the duty driver."

Well, I had no firm plans as to which way my night was going. I was only aiming for a pie and a pint in the pub and a phone call home, which at that time we could do from any phone box for half a crown. Actually, Northern Ireland was the only posting we ever had where we could do that, after all, it is part of the UK, even if it was a part where we got shot at.

Anyway, I started off from The Sailor's Rest and thought I would go straight over the hill and directly up to the school, avoiding William Street, after the recent fiasco when I took Webber up there a couple of weeks previously. But it didn't work out as I would have liked.

I am ashamed to say I got lost, something most unusual for me. I went over the hill and down into the valley and then I got turned around. Not a good thing to do in this neighbourhood, but I had an ace up my sleeve – my broad southern drawl. At that time, Yanks were popular in Derry as they were receiving prodigious amounts of arms and cash from America, and probably still are. But even so, I was lost in the worst possible place for a Brit soldier to get lost. My only course was to go back up the hill I had just come down, without attracting any undue attention.

When I got back up to the top, I could see both The Sailor's Rest and Rosemount and I got my bearings and headed back towards the school. I started down into the valley again and as I walked along I heard a voice behind me, and what he said was enough to make my blood run cold.

"We've been watching you, Brit," he said in that cold hard accent that you can never mistake. I was in between a rock and a hard place and if I couldn't bluff my way out I was a "dead man walking", as they were fond of saying in the Province. When I turned around there was three of "the boys" standing there watching me and I knew straight away that if I couldn't bluff my way out of this, if they believed I was a British soldier, I was finished.

I said, "What's a Brit, man?" in the broadest southern drawl I could muster.

The three of them stood there watching me and one of them piped up, "We thought you were with the Brits down in the town."

I laid on the drawl even thicker and said, "Do I sound like a Brit, man?"

I got the answer I was hoping for, "No, you don't, Yank," he said.

Now everything seemed to go in slow motion, time seemed to stand still. I wasn't armed and I knew they were. Two of them were convinced, but the third one wasn't. I wasn't sure about him but I still turned my back and tried to walk away. As I did, I felt like someone had pinned a target on my back and I carried on walking for about 100 yards, not daring to look back and hoping he would stay with the other two. But then I heard footsteps behind me and that damned hard flat Ulster accent.

"You're not a Yank, I've seen you down the town with them damned Brits!"

It was no good carrying on with the bluff, he knew who I was and as I turned to face him, he came at me with a knife. Now there was only one way out of this and I was lucky. If you ever have someone come at you with a knife, you want it to be by an amateur like him. He moved in with the knife held high for a downward thrust and basic unarmed combat made it simple and pretty easy to step in underneath it, turn him on his back and leave him lying in the road with his own knife in his throat. And if that sounds cold, well maybe it is, but he was trying to kill me and as cold as it sounds, it is still the best result for me.

But I still had the other two to deal with and luckily he had an old Beretta 9mm in his belt, which I quickly palmed and checked the load. Then I turned to the other two who decided as I was now armed and their spokesman was down and out of it, they had an urgent appointment elsewhere and they disappeared back into their alleyway.

I decided it was time for me to be elsewhere as well, in case they came back with more guns. So I didn't even report the incident, I just legged it for the school.

When I got there, seriously out of breath, the Redcap sergeant said, "What's up with you, Mac, you look a bit green around the gills?"

"Yeah, I was going for a pint but I don't feel so good now. I think I'll just go back to The Rest for an early night."

He said, "I've got a patrol going downtown. Jump in with them and they can drop you off."

I said, "Thanks, Sarge. I'll do that."

I was never so grateful for a lift in my life and I was soon back at The Sailor's Rest, without even making my phone call.

"What's up with you, Mac? I thought you were going for a pint," shouted Shelley.

"I've changed my mind, Sarge. I think I'll get some kip.

"Shit, someone call the doc, Mac must be ill!" shouted Shelley.

That was the last time we were allowed out in civvies in Derry, but I kept the old Beretta with me for the rest of the tour as 9mm ammo was easy to come by. I was a bit worried about taking it back to England, so I would give it a burial at sea on the ferry trip home.

Chapter Thirteen

The Smelly One in the Street

I was stretched out on my bunk in The Rest, contemplating a good book by Alistair McLean. It was a rest day; at least it was until someone decided to start a riot.

We did get quiet days like this sometimes. There would be an uneasy truce in the streets, until someone got knee-capped, or the Boys decided to rob a bank, or a sniper decided to have a go. It could sometimes get right boring in the streets.

We had a choice between dead boring, lazing about cleaning weapons, or cleaning rooms. Then there was the other side of the coin. A sudden burst of heart-stopping, adrenalin-filled action.

Anyway, I was fully engrossed in my book when Webber banged on my door and burst into the room like the force of nature that he is.

"Come on, Mac," he rumbled. "There is someone to see you in Parker's office!"

"Shit, who would want to see me, sir?"

We were pretty good friends by then, after all we had been through, but I still called him sir. He had earned that respect the hard way.

"Come on, Mac, you old bastard. The sooner you get in there, the sooner you'll find out."

I dragged myself out of my pit with as much interest as I could muster, which wasn't much as I never received mail from my family back in Seattle because of things that had happened years before that had completely split our family. In fact, as far as I knew, they didn't know that I was in the British Army. Anyway, I really could not work up any interest at all in any visitor that would want to see me.

I opened the door to the office and walked in to find the last person on earth that I wanted anything to do with. My father sat there in all his regalia. Major General Edwin T Mallory, US Army Rangers. His medal boards were wider than his chest and full of bullshit crackerjack medals. He was the one and only reason I had left America in the first place.

In fact, I did turn to walk out again but I came up against an extra door in the shape of Sergeant Major Webber, who filled the door so fully that there was no way to get past him.

I heard the bark of a demented dog behind me, "Sit down, Private Mallory!" the general snapped.

I turned my head and said wearily, "You're in the wrong army to give me orders, general."

The man seemed to deflate right before my eyes and he said weakly, "I'm sorry, Mac, please sit down."

Now that really was the shock of my life. I don't think the general had ever said please to anyone.

The memories came flooding back then of the years gone by when he bullied me, my younger brother Harry and even our mother, treating us like shit.

The general seemed to deflate even more, right before my eyes, if that was possible. Finally, he pulled himself together enough to start telling us the story.

He began falteringly, "As you guys probably know, the IRA usually conduct their fundraising tours around the Boston area, where they have a considerable following. Well, a few months ago they decided to try the Seattle area."

His voice was fading and he had to pause to collect his thoughts before he could continue. Finally he composed himself enough to carry on.

"Harry and some of his college friends were out on the town celebrating the completion of their exams and they decided that Shaunessy's Irish Bar downtown was as good a place as any to kick off their night on the town."

His voice was growing stronger and stronger as the story progressed.

"Things got more and more boisterous as the evening went on."

I said coldly, "Is there any point to all this, general? If so, could you please get to it because just listening to your voice is making me sick to my stomach and these guys can tell you, I have quite a strong stomach these days."

"Please, Mac, let me finish," he pleaded. "To cut it short, the boys had a row with these IRA men collecting for their cause and the bouncers had to separate the two groups. A couple of hours and a lot more drinks later, everyone thought the problems had been sorted. When closing time came, the boys were making their way to their car. Just then a car raced across the parking lot and crashed straight into the boys."

I knew what was coming now, but I had to hear it from him. Eventually he managed to get it out and the pain in his voice was obvious.

"Harry and three of his friends were dead when they got them to hospital."

I managed to say, "Did they find out who it was?"

He said, "The car was found abandoned later and although they couldn't prove it, they were positive the driver was one of your players here!"

All I could say was "who", in a strangled voice.

He said, "Eamon Driscoll."

I looked at Parker and he said, "Yes, Mac, our Eamon Driscoll. The local brigade commander for the Provos."

The general said, "Please, Mac, help me get the man who killed your brother."

"We've been after Driscoll for years, Mac, you know that. But he's a clever bastard," Webber said. "Yeah, he's Teflon, Mac. We can never make anything stick with him. He's probably responsible for at least ten security personnel deaths and we know he's responsible for a good part of the arms coming into the Province. He was responsible for the bomb at Ballymoney Police Barracks.

"The list just goes on and on," Webber said. "He lives across the border in Southern Ireland. Comes up here and wreaks havoc and then goes back south again. You know we can't go south after him, diplomatic crap and all that, we want this man as bad as the general, if not more, Mac."

I said, "Come on, sir, you've got 14 Company intelligence and the SAS. What the hell do you think I can do that they can't?"

"Come on, Mac, you know we can't use them. If anything goes wrong it will cause a diplomatic incident."

I said, "What you really mean is if you use me and everything goes tits up, it will be a deniable operation. An American serving in the British Army deserts to perform a revenge assassination on the IRA man who killed his brother in America. It's a win-win situation for the politicians back in Whitehall, and for the general here. If things go wrong it's my neck on the block, and if things go right, the spooks back at six get a man who has been on the top ten wanted list for the last three or four years. And, of course, the general here gets his revenge." I said. "It's a bit late to start worrying about your family after all these years, you old bastard."

"Please, Mac," he said. "I'm sorry for all I've done to our family. Can you ever forgive me?"

I said, "No, I don't think I can, you old bastard. If I agree to do this it will be for my boss here and for Harry. Not for you," and I waved towards Webber and Parker.

Once again he shrank into himself.

"I can live with that, Mac. Whoever you do it for doesn't matter, as long as you do it!"

Then I turned my back on him, dismissing him once again from my life. I turned to Webber and Parker and I said, "Okay. If we are going to do this, let's get on with it. I'll go out into the street as a down and out alcoholic. With my accent I'll probably get away with it. They love the Yanks here, as I found out when I took the kettle up to the Redcaps up at the Rosemount School. We'll need 14 Company in on this. I need to know when he's coming up here again, where he's going, what he's doing and who with. I'll have to take him in the street and make it look like just another old drunk with a gun. After all, everyone in this town has a gun. I presume you don't want him arrested, just to be let off by some United Nations court?"

They both said, "Yes, but we can't give you orders to that effect."

I said, "Okay. I'll get out into the streets as soon as possible. But remember, I need all the information I can get. I'm certainly not going to pop him down south. So we are going to need 14 Company on our side. I need two more things: first, I need the clothes of a tramp."

And right then I should have been forewarned by the gleam in Webber's eyes. Then he chuckled and said, "And second?"

I said, "In my kit I have a contraband item that I need the armourers to do some work on."

The big shit laughed out loud then and said, "You mean that poofy little Beretta you brought back from your little excursion up to Rosemount School with the kettle?"

I said, "Shit, how did you know about that?"

He laughed and said, "Come on, you old Yankee bastard, you should know by now that I know everything! What is it you want the armourer to do?"

I said, "I need a silencer fitted on it," and he just looked at me with a wicked gleam in his eye.

"Right. I'll see to it, old friend."

Just then the general piped up and said, "I can get you anything you want, just ask."

I just looked at him coldly. "I told you that if I did this job it would be for my boss here and for Harry. Your input is no longer required. Go back to America, you old parasite."

Then he got to his feet and slunk from the room like the beaten old man that he was.

Webber said, "Weren't you a bit hard on the old boy then, Mac?"

I said, "Like I told you, sir, you don't know what happened all those years ago."

He held his hands up and said, "Sorry, Mac. You're right, I don't know."

"Right. We need some dirty, smelly old clothes, the dirtier and the smellier the better, and I need to start sleeping in the street as soon as possible and when you can smell me before you can see me, we'll be getting there. Also, I'll need some sort of communication with you guys. I'll need information from 14 Company every day on Driscoll's whereabouts."

Webber said, "Don't worry, Mac, we'll be keeping an eye on you all the time."

"Hell, I might as well start as I mean to go on. I'll be bedding down in the back alley tonight."

Webber said, "Hang on, Mac. We found an old tramp dossing down in the railway sheds where we used to kip when we first got here." Then the big guy let out an evil laugh and said, "The old dosser gladly volunteered his best suit of clothes for you," and with that he held up a dirty, stinking, flea-ridden pair of ragged trousers and an equally smelly ragged shirt. The smell fairly made my eyes water.

"Shit!" I laughed. "Why do I think you're enjoying every minute of this?"

"Just one more thing, Mac," and the rumbling laugh came from deep in his chest. "I told you that we would look after you," he chuckled, and the last thing he produced was a scaly old First World War greatcoat. It was so dirty it could have stood up on its own. "Just one more thing," he laughed and then chucked the foul-smelling rag on the ground out in the back alley behind The Rest.

"Come on, boys!" he roared. "Let's put the finishing touches on Mac's disguise."

Then one by one, the boys lined up and pissed on my new coat, and every one of them was enjoying himself immensely. Now I really was The Smelly One from the Streets.

Gradually my beard grew and I got filthier and filthier as I moved from alleyway to alleyway and from garbage can to garbage can. I competed with the rats for a living, and eventually I was accepted as a regular, albeit filthy and smelly, fixture in the streets. To the local players I was just another tramp living rough in the streets; they took no notice of me or my accent. After all, a big part of their arms and money was coming from America. They wouldn't upset the apple cart by hurting me.

Every once in a while one of our patrols would pass by my latest five-star accommodation in a very posh cardboard box, in whichever back alleyway I had settled into the night before.

They would give me a kick as they passed by and throw me a packet of cold fish and chips from the local chippie, or whatever they got hold of, and give me a cheery, "Cop hold of that, you smelly old bastard" and as much as I enjoyed the cold greasy newspaper-wrapped offerings, it was really the information inside the packet that I really looked forward to. For this was the method that Webber had settled on to pass on the day-to-day intelligence collected by 14 Company.

After about two weeks of this routine, Dick Shelley came past one day and kicked my dirty foot sticking out of my luxury accommodation, and said, "Enjoy your grub, oh smelly one." Then under his breath as he passed by, he whispered, "Next Tuesday night, around 2200 hours, there will be an Army Council meeting in The Derry Arms, in the town square, and Driscoll will be there!"

I said, "Just make sure these kids know the score. I don't want to get shot by one of ours. A bullet is a bullet, whoever it comes from."

"Don't worry, Mac," he said. "Everyone has been briefed. You watch your back Tuesday night, we know he'll have at least two bodyguards and we don't know who else will be at the meeting."

I said, "And here I thought you guys were watching my back!"

Shelley and his patrol carried on up the alley and on their way. So I had another 48 hours to go in my five-star accommodation.

Then night fell and once more I faded into the background into the shadows where I belonged. After all, at night in the streets the safest place was in the shadows. But now I had to move on again as with the night came the regular inhabitants of the alley – rats as big as cats, and there was no way I was going to share my bed with them. It was too early to move to The Derry Arms yet, I had another 48 hours to go before the meeting so I had to find somewhere quiet and out of the way.

In the back alley behind the police station I found an old wreck of a car, left there after the last riots. The last place anyone would expect me to hide. I crawled into the front seat, wrapped myself in my smelly greatcoat and settled down for a long, cold, hungry night.

The next morning I had to move back to my five-star cardboard box and kick out the rats again as this was where the patrol would look for me and I had to be available when they came past with my breakfast and hopefully more information on Driscoll.

About ten in the morning Shelley once again brought the patrol past, gave me the obligatory kick in greeting and dropped a parcel of cold greasy chips and a meat pie – breakfast and dinner all in one.

"No change, Mac, the meeting is still at The Derry Arms at ten tomorrow night," he said under his breath. Then for the benefit of anyone that was taking an interest in the proceedings, he shouted, "Why don't you move along, you smelly old bastard!"

I said, "Okay, I'll hit them when they come out after the meeting. Make sure everyone is briefed and someone will have to watch my back in case more Provos leave at the same time as them."

"Okay, Mac. We'll have a sniper set up across the road, just in case."

Then they moved off down the road. I was alone again with the fleas and other assorted vermin. The rest of the day passed without incident and as night fell, I vacated The Ritz and left it to my scurrying, flea-ridden neighbours again and settled for another long, cold, hungry night in my Rolls Royce parked out the back of the police station.

Daybreak was slow in coming and when it finally did, I was glad to be into the last day of this job. I was looking forward to a shave, a haircut and at least an hour under a piping hot shower.

I moved down to the square to take up residence in the alleyway opposite The Derry Arms, so I could have eyes on, as they say.

It looked like being another long, hungry day, as it had been decided to keep the patrol away from me today in case we attracted attention from the wrong people. They would stay away from me unless they had to get some important information to me.

The day passed slowly into night, the time dragging so much that I was glad when the Army Council boys started to arrive. Then my heart started to pump and the adrenalin to flow when Driscoll and his oppos arrived.

I gave it another hour to let them get their meeting well under way, then I moved my cardboard box across the road close to the entrance of The Derry Arms and settled down to patiently await developments.

Eventually Driscoll and his two bodyguards exited the pub in front of me and the first bodyguard caught a whiff of me. I had been in the streets for about three weeks now and thanks to Webber and the boys preparing my clothes for me, I was smelly before I went into the streets and now I was downright putrid.

As he got the full force of the smell emanating from me, he turned to face me.

"God! Jesus, stand back, you smelly old bastard," he choked, as I staggered towards him offering my plastic bottle of White Lightning.

"Have a drink, buddy," I slurred as he stepped towards me to push me away. My silenced Beretta coughed twice and he went down in a heap in the road with a surprised look on his face. Bodyguard number two turned towards me and I could tell from the look in his eyes that he knew he was beaten, but he tried anyway. The Beretta coughed twice more and he too ended up like a bundle of discarded old clothes in the gutter, bleeding his life away.

Driscoll was kneeling on the road, hands on top of his head, crying, "Don't kill me! Please don't kill me!" he blubbered. The silencer on my Beretta was making a circular bruise in the soft flesh under his chin where I rammed it.

I said, "Look up! Look at me, you bastard! Look at me!" and the terror in his eyes was obvious. I said, "Four months ago you were in Seattle collecting money at Shaunessy's Bar in the city." I didn't ask him, I told him. "You had a row with some college boys," and he just looked at me warily. "You settled the argument by using your car as a battering ram. Four of them were DOA when they got them to hospital. One of them was my brother. Kiss your ass goodbye, mister!" and the Beretta coughed once more and blood, bone and brain matter splattered up into my face.

The next thing I knew, three Land Rovers screeched to a halt bottling me in. I dropped the gun in the road and my feet were kicked out from under me and I was kneeling in the road with my hands on my head. My hands were twisted behind me and the plasticuffs were put on.

The last thing I heard was Webber's hoarse whisper, "Jesus, Mac, you really do have a personal hygiene problem," as I was bundled unceremoniously into the back of a Land Rover.

We sped through the streets of Derry, with me flat on my face in the back and a size ten army boot planted firmly on the back of my neck.

The boys couldn't resist taking the piss out of me as we went.

"God you stink, Mac. Time for a regimental bath for you. Bass broom and Vim for you, Yank," went the banter.

But for all that, I knew I was amongst friends and I could relax. I hadn't slept properly for about three weeks now and it was all catching up with me. When we finally pulled up at the gates of RAF Ballymoney, I had actually dozed off.

The boys in the back were nudging me back and forth and I heard an amazed voice say, "The old bastard has gone to sleep! Come on, Mac, wake up. Are you bored with all this?"

I heard Webber in the front chuckling, "Come on, Mac, you old bastard, what have we got to do to keep you entertained?"

The gate guard must have been expecting us because we weren't kept waiting long and we were rushed through to the sergeants' mess accommodation. As the Brits said, I wasn't posh enough for the five-star stuff, the officers' mess.

We pulled up with a screech of brakes and I was dragged out of the Land Rover by my ankles. These boys were never going to be accused of being to gentle with a prisoner.

Quickly I was dragged inside and I was encouraged to see the boys taking up posts all around the Land Rovers, keeping the curious RAF bods at arm's length.

When we got inside I found black plastic bags and clean clothes of the civilian persuasion.

Webber said, "Come on, Mac, we don't have much time, get out of those flea-ridden rags."

I laughed and said, "What, don't I get any privacy here?"

Quickly I stripped off the rags, which were dumped in the bags and taken straight off to the incinerator and then I headed for the showers, where I spent a good hour delousing, defleaing and shaving off my grotty beard. As soon as I left the shower, I was pushed into a chair and attacked by the airbase barber.

After about 15 minutes I was shorn and I started to dress in the civvies. Less than two hours after we got there, I was once more bundled out and back into the Land Rover, looking like a completely different person to the tramp that had arrived there such a short time ago. This time Webber was in the back with me.

He said, "Right, Mac, listen up. We don't have much time. I presume your passport is back at The Rest with your gear?"

I said, "Yeah, it's all back there."

"Right, Mac, I'll take care of all that. Now this is what's going to happen. You're going to be flown to RAF Brize Norton where you'll catch a C130 Hercules that will take you to RAF Akrotiri. On both flights, from here and from Brize Norton, the crews will be told to leave you alone. The less they know about what happened here the better.

"Once we get you out of the country and away from the nosey press, all you have to do is have a nice holiday in Cyprus. We'll circulate rumours that you are something to do with Special Forces. That will be enough so they don't take too close an interest in you. There will be rumours, there always are, but they'll leave you to it."

I said, "What about passport and visa?"

"Not necessary," he said. "You won't be leaving the sovereign base area. Then it's only a matter of topping up your suntan till things quieten down here. We'll circulate rumours that it was a UDR hit, which is not a long stretch of the imagination as these guys are mortal enemies. If they don't swallow that, we'll go for the first scenario, just another drunk with a gun in a city where everyone has a gun. Once things have quietened down here, we'll go for your RTU, return to unit."

"Just make it as quick as possible, sir," I said.

Webber repeated, "As quick as possible, old friend. We need you back here."

A quick trip out onto the tarmac took us to a Wessex helicopter that was waiting for us. As I shook hands with the big bugger, I said, "Don't forget how easily I get bored, sir."

He laughed and said, "Shit, the last thing we want is for you to get bored, you old fart," then I was in the noisy interior of the big old Wessex workhorse helicopter.

Webber was right, the crew had been told to leave me alone, not like my last flight to Aldergrove when I was the VIP passenger. I signalled the loadie for a set of ear defenders and surprisingly, I actually got some sleep, and if you have ever had a flight in a Wessex, you'll know how hard that is.

After a refuel stop, which I can't tell you anything about because, unbelievably, I was asleep – Webber would have been proud of me – we finally arrived at RAF Brize Norton, where we found a Hercules waiting for us.

I was quickly transferred to the Hercules, along with the company of the Queen's Regiment on their way to Sharjah to take up the posting there; another place I had been and I had no wish to return amongst the flies.

Webber was true to his word and after they had checked me out, as soldiers do, they took no further interest in me for the duration of the flight. On the stopover at Akrotiri for refuelling, I was the only passenger to disembark.

I was met by an RAF flight sergeant in an unusually blue Land Rover – I was used to the green machines of the infantry. I threw what little kit I had in the back of the blue Land Rover and said to the blue sergeant, "I hope there is more kit here for me because I have come with fuck all really!"

He said, "Don't worry, sir, I have to take your sizes and shop for more kit for you tomorrow."

I thought, if he's calling me sir, he really has been told a story about me.

Within ten minutes he pulled up at the sergeants' mess accommodation block and told me to jump out there and that I would have my accommodation at cabin number five. Shit these RAF boys know how to live, no barrack rooms for them.

He said, "I'll be back at 1000 hours tomorrow with your kit."

I said, "You realise I don't have any money with me?"

"Don't worry, sir," he said. "I've been told all your expenses will be picked up by the MOD and all your meals will be delivered here for the duration of your stay. You can use the gymnasium at certain times and you are allowed to run the inside of the camp perimeter at any time of the day or night, that will suit your job. But you won't be allowed to mix with the base personnel at any time."

I wondered what he had been told about my job and I said jokingly, "No chance of a quick pint in the mess, then?"

The time passed slowly and I was truly bored after a couple of weeks, though I really shouldn't have been, I was in one of the most beautiful places in the world and I should have been able to relax and make a holiday of it. But I just couldn't, it was the same old boring routine day after day: eat, sleep, run and lay in the sun. I was itching to get back to Derry with the boys.

One morning when I was returning from my first run, ready for a shower and my breakfast, I found a suit waiting for me by the front door. His opening conversation was a bore from the start.

He said, "Do you know who I am?"

What an arrogant prat this was.

I said, "No, but I know what you are. You are a spook from Box."

"Yes, I am and we can use someone of your abilities."

I said, "Yeah, I know. You want me to do all your dirty jobs until the shit hits the fan and then you'll drop me like a hot potato."

He said, "You are probably right, but for your talents I can get you the big bucks."

"What good are the big bucks to me, buddy, when things go tits up? And things are bound to sometime. You'll shit on me as soon as look at me."

He said, "Private Mallory, you've got a real talent for our work."

I said, "I know, but I don't want to work for you. Your top spook is a politician and I don't trust them. I just want my RTU, a return to unit."

He said, "I could leak details of what you have done in Derry and make things very awkward for you."

"Look, son," I replied, "if you're going to threaten me, you need to check your facts. There are a lot of people over in Derry who have gone to great lengths to blame that job on the Ulster Defence Regiment. If you leak the truth, there will be a lot of pissed off people on both sides off the water, politicians in Whitehall and even your head spook at Box. And lucky you, they will all be pissed off at you."

He looked at me thoughtfully for 30 seconds before making the only decision possible.

He said, "Okay, but just remember, no one likes a smart-ass." His parting shot was, "Enjoy the rest of your holiday. You can expect your new orders to come through any day now."

After another week passed by, running, eating, sleeping and staying away from the base gym as they only wanted me there after hours, I was getting really bored.

One day, my flight sergeant finally brought me the news I was waiting for when he brought my breakfast.

"Good news, Mac, you're on a flight out of here in 48 hours. Back to Brize where you'll join a draft of replacements bound for Belfast and Derry. You've finally got your RTU." He laughed, "I know how bored you were here."

I said, "Thank Christ for that. I mean, this is a nice place for a holiday and a suntan, but only if you can go off the base. I was that close to getting cabin fever here."

He went out the door chuckling so much that he reminded me of Webber.

The next two days passed slowly and finally it was time to pack up my meagre gear and my chauffer picked me up and deposited me at the noisy Hercules again. Finally we took off for Blighty, as my Brit colleagues called home. Once again, ear defenders on, I settled down to the long, noisy, vibrating journey back to Brize Norton.

Once again the loadie left me to my own devices till finally he shook me awake at Brize and pointed me towards a Wessex on the tarmac.

As I left the now quiet Herc, I heard him mumble, "Special Forces. Shit, they can sleep on a clothes-line!" That brought a sleepy grin to my face.

I finally stumbled out of one noise-maker and into another, where the loadie wordlessly gave me another set of ear defenders and pointed me towards a corner seat at the back.

In the front there were four rookies looking out of sorts and out of place, but I didn't have the inclination to reassure them as I settled into my seat and promptly drifted off to sleep again. They were heading into the unknown, but I was going home. Maybe I could be bothered to show them the ropes at the end of our journey. But not just now. I was determined to get back to the dream I'd been immersed in, about the lovely nurses back at Aldergrove Hospital. Webber would have been proud of me.

Chapter Fourteen

Town Patrol

When we had done our stint in the streets, we would pull back to our five-star holiday camp at McGilligan Point, an old Second World War POW camp, which was where we had our R&R, or rest and recuperation. When I say five star, that's with tongue definitely in cheek, it was more like minus five star. Still, it was our home for the rest period, even though the shower block had a sign over the door saying "Save water and bath with a friend". This was testament to our inadequate hot water supply.

As I said, McGilligan was a run-down Second World War POW camp situated out on McGilligan Point, which meant that we had the Irish Sea on three sides and in the winter it was damp and colder than a Witch's tit.

When we were billeted at McGilligan, all we had to relieve the boredom was camp guard – which I can tell you was no relief at all – the odd fishing trip, or town patrol. Now Town Patrol was one Land Rover with driver and whichever warrant officer or senior sergeant who couldn't move fast enough to avoid getting rostered onto it.

But I have to say it was marginally less boring than being confined to our illustrious POW camp. If I was pulled as the driver, it meant I had to chauffeur whichever warrant officer or senior sergeant had been caught, on a magical mystery tour around Coleraine and the surrounding districts.

I was armed with my SLR and extra magazines, and my passenger would carry a shitty old Canadian Browning Hi-Power 9mm automatic that has to go down as one of the most useless handguns ever issued to the British Army. Not a massive amount of firepower considering what the terrs had in their arsenal and I still have to wonder why we never lost one of these patrols considering what we were up against. It would have been so easy for the boys to get together and take us out. If we got hit, we were in radio contact but we wouldn't have seen any help for at least half an hour, and possibly longer.

We came close one night when I was driving a staff sergeant called Simpson. He had a girlfriend living on a farm outside Coleraine and his idea of a good patrol was for me to drive around doing wheelies on the frozen roads and then taking him to the farmhouse where his girlfriend lived so he could get his leg over while I sat outside in the Land Rover freezing with the brass monkeys.

He finally came out about one in the morning.

"You all right, Mac," he said.

"Yeah I'm just peachy keen, Sarge, freezing my nuts off," I said. "Next time we do town patrol, can you get her to bring her sister?"

All I got from him was a laugh and he said, "Let's get on with this patrol so we can get back to camp and get some sleep."

Well, I pulled away from the farmhouse, thinking about a late supper in the cookhouse followed by a warm bed, when it happened. As we came to the first intersection, a car screeched to a halt in front of us. Now they say a soldier's life on active service can be described as long periods of complete boredom punctuated by short periods of pure terror and adrenalin overloads, and I have to say this is absolutely true.

As the car pulled up in front of us, I could see there were four guys in it and they were armed. I pulled the wagon up on a handbrake turn, swinging to the right so that Simpson was facing the car full of soldiers of the revolution. Luckily Simpson was on the ball and he had the Browning out and was pumping bullets into the car as fast as he could pull the trigger.

The next problem was another car full of the boys with guns was tearing up behind us and I couldn't get to my gun in the rack behind my seat, I was too busy driving and to stop just then would have been tantamount to suicide, so I thought it was time for a bit of cross-country. They had me boxed in a narrow country lane.

Now I don't care how good you are with a saloon car on normal roads, you have no chance against a British Army Land Rover in the hands of someone who has been on the government vehicle testing grounds near Pirbright.

So I whacked it into four-wheel drive and headed across the fields with the pedal to the metal, as they say. Of course, the boys tried to follow me and as soon as they hit the farmer's field they were both bogged down.

So several very frustrated Provos were left stuck in the farmers field taking potshots at a rapidly disappearing Land Rover with no lights on.

Simpson said, "Damn, boy, that was pretty good driving!"

I said, "I didn't spend all that time racing around the testing grounds for nothing. And by the way, I just hope she was worth it."

He sat back in the seat chuckling. "Yeah. You know what? She really was."

"Well, I hope so," I said. "Because you can fill in all the paperwork and do all the reports, including ammunition expended and the bullet holes in my Land Rover. And you'll have to think about what we were doing off our patrol area. And one more thing."

"Yeah, what's that?" he said.

"Just how did they know we were there?"

He thought about it for a second and then he laughed and said, "You know what? It was still worth it."

Chapter Fifteen

The Night of the Pigs

My first Saturday night back with the boys turned out to be one of our worst ever of the tour. We had gone through the usual welcome back, when Webber was on form with the wind-ups. With, "Jesus, Mac, you smell better. Did they give you a bath while you were on holiday?" and, "Where's that smelly old bastard we sent away?" I as back amongst friends. I was glad to be back in the streets.

We always knew when we were in for a bad night. First the order would come around to leave our berets behind and put on our skid lids or steel helmets, and if they called out the pigs, the Saracen armoured cars, well, then we knew we were in for a very serious night.

That night we could hear the crackle of small arms' fire and the rumble of the explosions. So far nothing out of the ordinary, but we were all waiting for the call to go and clear up the mess.

When the call finally came through, we were told some firemen were in trouble up at the top of William Street, where they had been called to deal with a fire started by some rioters.

Now this was par for the course for these boys, until they arrived on the scene and promptly came under fire from the Black Balaclava Boys. Now these guys were used to having the odd brick chucked at them, but when the shooting started they very sensibly handed over to us. When the bullets started to fly we were called in to deal with the situation. Once we had cleared the area the firemen could get on with their job.

It turned out to be an ambush for us. The boys were waiting for us to roll up in our soft-skinned Land Rovers and we were welcomed by fire from an AK47.

Well, now it was time to call in the heavy gang and three pigs eventually rolled up to where our advance was halted and we were crouched behind our Land Rovers, which were absolutely no use when it came to stopping bullets.

The heavy duty grey armoured Land Rovers were not deployed until long after we left the Province. Of course, your first instinct when the bullets started to fly was not one of excitement, not unless you were unhinged, but your instinct was to get behind something solid that would stop a bullet, and that thing was not our old Land Rovers.

When the bullets start to fly, anyone who says they enjoy getting shot at is full of shit and there is something really comforting about these lumbering piles of iron going up the road in front of you.

It is not the people who go into a streetfight like that not feeling any fear who are the brave ones, it is those who are nearly crippled by fear but can force themselves to get up and advance, even if it is behind an ugly old pig on wheels. These are the real brave ones.

Just then Webber came up the road laughing and shouting. We were still crouched behind our Land Rovers. The pigs had rolled through and formed up three abreast in front of us – a solid bullet-proof wall of cast iron on wheels. Those three monsters each disgorged a section of infantry that formed up in line across the road behind the protecting pigs.

Then Webber was there adding his bulk to the iron wall in front of us.

"Come on, Mac, you old Yankee bastard. What are you doing hiding down there? Come on, you buggers. We've got a road to clear of AK47s so the boys from the fire brigade can get on with their job. Form up with the pig passengers and let's get on with it."

And he shouted at me as he went past, "Look after the new boy with you."

I looked down at the frightened face of the young lad crouching there, behind the front wheel of my Land Rover. Good boy, I thought, a fast learner. He had the safest place there; he had the engine block and the front wheel in between him and the 7.62 shorts that were coming our way.

As I looked down at him, I smiled. "You are a fast learner, son. What's your name?"

"My name is Sammy Gerard," he faltered.

I said, "Well, Sammy, you see that big shit that just went past shouting his mouth off and laughing?"

"Yes," he said. "A bit of a clown, is he?"

I said, "Jesus, boy, you have just made the biggest mistake possible in this madhouse! If you listen to everything that big shit says, and do everything he says when he says it, you might just survive to make the trip home from this circus sitting upright instead of in a body-bag."

The boy said, "I'm sorry, Mac, I didn't know."

"Well, know now and don't apologise. You have nothing to apologise for. Come on, get up into line behind this rolling scrap iron. Take notice. Webber is your best chance of survival in this madhouse and these ugly buggers run a close second."

So we were up and moving behind the protective pigs while the bullets continued to buzz around us like a multitude of demented bees. The only problem with this was we could move forward and clear the road easily enough, but the big boys that we were following could not clear the snipers settled in with their AK47s on the upper floors of the houses that we were passing.

We had to do that the hard way, with house to house clearance, the hardest and most bloody job we were ever called upon to do. So we could only advance behind our cast iron friends and then we had to clear out the shooters the hard way.

I pulled young Sammy up into line with me and we started to move forward.

Suddenly a 7.62 round ricocheted off the iron pig in front of us. I had a quick look at the high windows on either side of us and I didn't see a shooter. This was a bad thing in this situation; you don't usually get a second chance, but this time we did, although young Sammy didn't. The next shot hit him in the side and the bullet took in layers of nylon from his flak vest resulting in a wound twice as bad as it should have been.

I didn't have time to look to Sammy because at that instant, I saw a rifle barrel poking out a second floor window. Instantly, I sent a double tap through the offending window and the rifle barrel disappeared sharply.

Then I had time to check Sammy and he was in a bad way. Not only did he have to put up with the bullet wound, but he also had to put up with the mess caused by the nylon.

I shouted for a medic then I had to leave him and rejoin the line advancing behind the pigs. He was in the hands of the medics now.

Our protective line of iron crept along the road, clearing our way but whenever we came to a house with a sniper in it they had to stop and wait till we had cleared the house, we couldn't leave them behind us, or our iron friends were no longer any use to us as cover, because the snipers could fire at us from behind.

When it came to house clearance it was usually Webber kicking in the door and me coming in behind him, to take out anyone that threatened our human bulldozer. But sometimes we could talk the big guy into letting someone else go in first. Sometimes Dick Shelley would go first, sometimes me, but we progressed up William Street, with the pigs clearing the road and then us clearing houses the hard way.

We leapfrogged up the road like this, with either Webber first, or me, or Shelley, followed by a team of three following to clear up the mess. In this way we cleared the road house by house and room by room.

But I have to say, going through the door first was one of the hardest things I ever had to do in my time in the British Army. When you kicked in that door you didn't know what or who to expect on the other side. I would much rather follow the big bugger or Shelley in and then pick off anyone waiting for us.

As we rolled up William in this fashion, we finally came abreast with the fires that we were here for in the first place, and the firemen could get on with their job.

Suddenly a 7.62 short from an AK47 ricocheted off the pig in front of me and bounced off and took out the man beside me, and I'm ashamed to say I didn't even know his name. He was one of the original crew that had come up with the pig.

Now came the hard part. Someone had to go in and clear that house room by room before we could advance another foot, so the pigs rolling in front of us ground to a halt.

Now it was our turn and I was up. Shelley and Webber had cleared the last two snipers. Now it was my turn again.

"Mac!" shouted Webber. "Pick your crew."

Now this was sometimes a problem. I had no rank because I refused to take it. This was an old problem that dated back to the general ordering me to go to West Point, and me refusing and leaving home.

But what I lacked in rank I made up for with experience, and one thing these boys respected was experience in the field, and that experience gained me the full trust and respect of these boys. Well, most of them anyway. In fact, there was so much respect that I didn't have to pick them, they would actually volunteer, and that was saying something as this was the worst job that they would ever have to do. And I have to say, that this goes against all their training, as in the British Army you never volunteer for anything.

So when Webber shouted for me to pick a crew, the boys lined up with me. Two of our hard-nuts were first: Joey Davis and Dave McAuley, and I was glad to see them. They would be numbers two and three through the door behind me. Number two breaking left and number three breaking right, and hopefully they would take out anyone waiting for us and give me time to bring my weapon to bear after I had smashed through the door.

I needed one more volunteer to back them up and a Brummie called George Garry stepped forward and he had an evil glint in his eye. Garry had a thing about foreigners in the British Army and he hated my guts. This was not normally something that worried me unduly, but there was no way on earth that I wanted him behind me with a loaded gun when I went through that door. It was more than likely that his first bullet would end up in my back.

I called Webber over and he said, "Are you ready, Mac?"

I said, "Yeah, I'm ready, sir. But I won't go through that door with Garry behind me. He has a pathological hatred for all foreigners and his first bullet will probably be for me."

Webber took in the situation at a glance and said, "That bad hey?"

I said, "Yes, I think it is. He's got a thing about foreigners in his army!"

Webber could have made a big thing of it, but he trusted me, and I could see from the look in his eye we had enough water under the bridge to know that I would never pull a stunt like this if it wasn't absolutely necessary. The big bugger stood up for me straight away.

"Okay, you useless load of buggers!" he roared. "The order of march on is Mac through the door first, Davis and McAuley are numbers two and three, and yours truly is number four because I need the practice," and his booming laugh even drowned out the noise of the small arms' fire and the explosions temporarily. And no one would dare to argue with him, especially Garry, who just gave me an evil look as he slunk off, and I knew this was not over by a long chalk.

"Come on, Mac, you're in charge now," boomed the big shit.

I handed my SLR to the nearest radio operator, who was struggling to make his Pioneer work.

"Lend me your SMG will you, Smitty. I need a short gun for a while."

We lined up in the cover of the nearest cast iron pig.

"Right, guys," I said. "We need to clear number 42 and we know there's at least one AK in there and we don't know what else. It's me first with the sledge and then it's Davis and McAuley left and right and then the boss is number four."

Davis and McAuley couldn't conceal their surprise or their relief when they knew that Webber was to be number four through the door behind them.

All this had taken place quickly, after the first shot from number 42, the house that we were about to clear.

I checked out the SMG. It had two 30-round magazines taped back to back, more than I would need for this job. Davis and McAuley checked their weapons and I could see from the look on their faces that they were pumped up with adrenalin and ready for whatever was to come. There was no need to check on Webber, he was always ready.

This was it, time for me to summon the steel for my backbone to go with the steel in the sledge I was carrying. I checked the team behind me, then focused all my attention on the door. I hit it on the run and the weight I put behind the sledge carried me through the door and on into the living room.

Davis and McAuley were right behind me. I was reassured by the sound of Davis's SLR barking as he took out the first gun on the landing. Things were definitely going noisy and we were hoping that was the only gun we had to deal with, but we were not going to be that lucky.

Davis had taken out the first gun on the first floor, but we couldn't be sure that was the only one. I went straight through and out into the kitchen. I had no doubt that Davis and McAuley would handle anything on the upper floors.

As I crashed through, suddenly I was taking fire from the back garden.

A bullet burned past my neck, and luckily it was only a graze, no matter how much it burned.

When I crashed through into the back garden, I was suddenly confronted by a young girl with an AK47 and I have to say, for the first time in Derry, I froze. This was not like me at all; I never froze on the job. But then this was the first time I'd had to face a young girl with a gun. When she threw down on me she would have killed me, but luckily I had the big guy behind me and before she could squeeze the trigger, Webber's SLR exploded, putting three rounds centre mass and her chest was shredded and she was thrown backwards over the rose beds.

I was still frozen in the same position when Webber's bulk hit me in the back.

"Come on, you old bastard, wake up. She would have killed you."

I shook my head. I was in a daze, but he was right, if it wasn't for the fact I had Webber as my number four, I would be making the trip back to England in a body bag. Davis and McAuley came down the floors shouting, "Top floors clear, Mac!" and Webber was looking at me as if to say, get it together and clear the rest of this house.

Just then the door to the cellar opened and a player with an M16 burst out. My SMG jumped in my hand as I emptied a 30-round magazine through the cellar door, sending him tumbling back down.

Just then the big shit piped up with, "Welcome back, Mac. I think you can declare this house well and truly cleared now."

But someone still had to go down those stairs, to make sure he was the only one. What we were doing here was classed as a police action, so I wasn't allowed to throw a grenade down and do it the easy way, even if it was the best way to clear the cellar. This was my gig so it was me that had to take the long walk down the stairs.

I looked at Webber and he raised his eyebrows at me as if to say, do you want me to do it? I said, "No, it's my turn so I'll do it."

I didn't have to open the door as there wasn't a lot left of it after the long burst of 9mm I had put through it. Luckily the lights were still on and I could see what I was walking into and what looked like a bundle of old clothes sprawled in disarray at the bottom of the stairs. The difference was, even from up here I could see the blood seeping out onto the cellar floor.

The smell of cordite was strong enough to turn my stomach as I started down the stairs with the reassuring presence of the big bugger right behind me.

Luckily, there was nowhere for a gunman to hide and we cleared the cellar in quick time.

As we turned to go back up the stairs, I bent down to pull the balaclava from the torn and bleeding body lying there and I immediately regretted my actions. I felt like I had just had a sharp blow to the solar plexus and my mouth went dry. The face I revealed wouldn't have been out of place on a choir boy.

I looked at Webber and even *he* had nothing to say except, "Come on, Mac, let's get out of here." And that was said uncharacteristically quietly for the big guy.

As we came out of the cellar the look on our faces must have told a story.

McAuley said, "What's up, boss?"

"Think yourself lucky that you cleared the upper floors," said Webber, and left it at that. I just stumbled out the door looking for fresh air. Some days our job was just so much shit.

But there was no point in feeling sorry for ourselves, we still had to clear the rest of the bloody street, one way or another.

So we formed a line behind our rolling iron wall and got on with the job. Webber came down the line doing his usual job, keeping us on our toes and our morale up.

"You all right, Mac?" he said.

"Yeah, I'm all right, boss. Same old shit, different day. Our job is just peachy, isn't it, sir?"

Then the big bugger actually laughed and said, "You are getting old, Mac. Come on, we've had worse days than this. I can't afford to have you going sour on me."

And I had to agree with him, things could always get worse.

You know how they say be careful what you wish for because you might just get it, well, we got it and things suddenly got much, much worse.

From the front up the road, suddenly there was a loud whoosh and we were rocked by a violent explosion as an RPG, a rocket propelled grenade, took the left hand front wheel from the pig on the left of the line and put it through the living room window of the house nearest to it.

Unfortunately, it decapitated the soldier on the left of the line on its way, leaving a trail of blood and gore behind. This day was getting better and better. The driver was lucky and he managed to scramble from the burning pig before the flames reached him. Things were getting decidedly messy and this was what we meant when we said things had gone loud.

We found out later that a man and a woman were in the living room at the time, watching proceedings, and when the wheel landed in the living room they were killed instantly. Terrorists anywhere in the world never have been bothered about what they euphemistically call collateral damage.

There were two GPMGs in the line and both gunners emptied a full belt of 7.62 at the offending window the RPG had fired from, reducing the surrounding area of the wall to smoking rubble.

It certainly looked like the RPG had been taken out, but we couldn't be sure. Someone would still have to go in and clear the house the hard way, just as soon as we got ourselves reorganised after the devastating explosion that had taken out our left-hand pig and scattered us like ninepins! The medics were going to have a busy time after this job was finished.

We finally got ourselves sorted out and advanced up the road again, until we came to the bullet-riddled house that the RPG had been fired from.

Now came the house clearance again. I had done the last one so this was down to Webber or Shelley. Straight away Webber decided to do this one and he took the lead again.

"Want me on this one, sir?" I said. After all, he'd backed me up on the last one.

"Okay, Mac. You're number two," and straight away the two wide boys, Davis and McAuley, jumped in feet first.

"We'll come, boss," they chimed in, and I for one was glad they had volunteered. It was always good to have them behind you and I could tell from the grin on his face that Webber was in agreement.

"Right, you buggers!" he shouted. "Come on, let's get this done."

As usual Webber hit the door like a rampant bull, all but destroying it. Through the door he went with me right behind him going left. Davis went right, with McAuley bringing up the rear. We were met by a silent, empty house, but we all knew that meant nothing.

"Come on, Mac, you and me upstairs. You two clear the ground floor." This to Davis and McAuley.

We moved carefully up the stairs with me covering the big bugger's back. We entered the front bedroom with not a little trepidation and my first impression was that we had walked into an abattoir.

Flesh and blood and bone splinters, all that was left of the two men that had fired the RPG at us, were scattered all round the bedroom. They had borne the full brunt of two full belts of 7.62 from the two GPMGs and the result wasn't pretty. It was shocking, even to us, and we saw this kind of carnage every day. Anyway, they would never be firing RPGs at us again. There was hardly enough left of them for the medics to collect and put in their rubber body bags. All we could do then was to clear the other rooms, and we found nothing.

When we went downstairs. McAuley's report was a terse "All clear, boss. Anything up there?"

"Nothing that will be giving us any more trouble," growled Webber. And after one look at his face, they had no more questions.

We formed up the line again, albeit with only two pigs this time, and moved on up to the end of the street. We encountered no more opposition. As it had happened so many times before, they'd had enough and the Balaclava Boys melted away into the night.

Now to clear up the mess, which always fell to us, and this time part of the mess was a burnt out pig. The fire department had finally got to the fires and done their job, thanks to our boys. Now came the worst part of the job, totting up the butcher's bill. Four of our boys would be going home in body bags, three would be evacuated to England with severe bullet and shrapnel wounds, and one with third-degree burns from being too close to the pig when it brewed up. We also had seven walking wounded that could be treated by our medics here, involving nothing more than bandages and light duties.

All in all an expensive night for us, but I didn't want to say things could easily be worse, because as in the case of our brewed up pig, they easily could.

Chapter Sixteen

Death of a Longhair

It was about 2200 hours and I'd just had a hot drink and an egg banjo in the canteen, and was heading back to my room with every intention of curling up with a good book for an hour and hopefully getting a good night's sleep. I wasn't down for any duty till 0800 hours, when I was down for a foot patrol.

Suddenly the late night peace and quiet of The Rest was shattered by a roar from the large one.

"Mac!" he shouted. So much for the quiet night with the book.

I quickly changed direction and headed for Webber's office. As I went through the door, I said, "You bellowed, oh large one."

"Don't be cheeky, you old Yankee bastard," but despite the room shaking, he already had the beginnings of a grin creeping onto his face. "Get your wagon warmed up and ready to go, Mac, we've got to make a quick trip down to the town square. The foot patrol has found a body and we have to attend, along with the RUC."

When I pulled the Land Rover over to The Rest, Webber jumped in the front and Sergeant Gerry Anderson and two privates jumped into the back. They would act as escort and we would use the foot patrol to secure the area where the body was found when we got to the square.

It took only a couple of minutes to make the short drive from The Rest to the square and I pulled up behind the grey RUC Land Rover. Webber sent Gerry to take command of the foot patrol and secure the area.

"Come on, Mac, let's go and have a look," and he shook hands with the RUC sergeant as they greeted each other. I had a quick look at the shabbily dressed body; his hands were tied behind his back and he looked for all the world like a down and outer, a street tramp.

He had a small entrance hole on one side of his head and there was a mess of blood, brain and bone fragments scattered around on the ruined exit side, or what was left of it.

He was lying on his side and he had a square of cardboard on a string hanging around his neck. There was some writing on it but as he was half laying on it, I could only make out part of what it said.

I took the ever-present stiletto out of my pocket and pressed the button that released the blade with a click. By now Webber and the boys were taking an interest in the proceedings. I used the knife to tease the rest of the sign into view.

It read "Fuck off home you Brit bastards". I was starting to get a sick feeling in the pit of my stomach.

I took a closer look at his head and his ravaged face. Shit, I knew who this guy was.

"Do you recognise him, sir?" I asked Webber.

"Shit," he growled, "yes, I do!"

There was no doubt, it was Captain Stephens from 14 Company. He had been trussed up like a chicken and executed by the Black Balaclava Boys. This was no way for a soldier to die. He was one of ours; a soldier doing one of the most dangerous jobs in the Province.

If we didn't find whoever had done this quickly and take him down hard, they would be doing this again. I looked at Webber.

"Jesus, boss. If we don't catch this bastard quick, you know what this will do to our street cred. Like you said before, we live on our street cred here. Shit, it's what keeps us alive!"

"I know, Mac, this is as bad as it gets. None of our street guys will be safe ever again if we don't sort this out now!"

We left our foot patrol to clear up things in the square and headed back to The Rest.

It was a quiet, thoughtful crew that filed back into the canteen and Webber went in to report to Parker. We sat there drinking our tea or coffee, each alone with our thoughts.

Finally Gerry was the first one to find his voice.

"Do any of you guys realise how serious this is?"

Before anyone could reply, Webber and Parker came out of the office.

"Right, guys, listen up for the major," growled the big shit.

Then Parker started in. "I think you lads realise the seriousness of what has happened tonight. We've got to sort this out quickly or the Provo hard men will be trying this again and again. All our lads out in the streets will be vulnerable and our intelligence will dry up altogether! Shortly, 14 Company will bring us a list of local players and we will start kicking in doors on one of the biggest manhunts ever mounted in the Province and we won't stop till we find the bad boys that executed our man. We will go out in six-man teams and each will be allocated a target. Once you have arrested your man, you will transport him to McGilligan where we will have interrogation teams waiting to sweat them, and we can and we will hold them for 36 hours. We'll keep the pressure on until someone cracks and gives us the information that we want."

This was the longest speech we'd ever had from Parker. Then Webber added his two cents worth.

"Get some rest, boys. As soon as we get the information we are waiting for we'll start chasing them and we don't stop until we find the bastards that killed our boy, so you won't be getting much sleep at all. And we take the gloves off for this one. Sod the yellow card and the politicians in Whitehall. This one's personal and these bastards made it that way."

The rules had been made; we were going take these bastards down hard and fast. They would think long and hard before taking out one of our plain clothes boys in the street! If Webber was this pissed off with them, this was really going to get messy!

The blitz started at midnight that night and we had every intention of keeping up the pressure till someone cracked and gave up the scrotes that we were after.

I was on a team with Gerry Anderson and five other guys. We were sent after a local hard man called Danny Brady. We went out in two Land Rovers and I was driving one and a guy called Dave Stanley was to drive the other.

In the briefing, Gerry had given us the "SP" on this scrote!

"Right, guys, this Brady is one of the real bad boys! If he didn't actually kill our boy Captain Stephens, he'll know who did, but he won't come easy! He lives on a little farm just outside of Derry. He probably won't be on his own when we take him and don't forget what the large one said, this one is heavy duty and don't worry about the yellow card."

We pulled up on the main road about 200 yards from the turning into his farm. We could see the lights down at the bottom of the hill.

"Shit, Gerry, it looks like he's still up. This could get noisy!"

"Yeah, Mac. You got any suggestions?"

"Yes," I said. "It would be nice to have the small soldiers here, this is right up their street. But we don't, so what do you think of this Danny? Let me go down and have a closer look and then we can work out something to make this a shitty night for him."

"Okay, Mac. Do you want some help?"

"No, you know I'm better off operating on my own in the dark."

"Yeah, I know, your Indian blood shows in a situation like this."

I worked my way down to the farmhouse slowly and when I got close enough, I could see he had two 4x4s parked in the yard. Then I worked my way closer and got a look in the window.

What I saw then pleased me no end. Brady was stretched out on the couch half naked and partying hard with two naked Colleens. There were open bottles of Jack Daniels on the table and from what I could see, there were lines of white powdery stuff on any available flat surface.

I could only see the three of them, so it looked like Brady was totally secure in his little farmhouse. Although I couldn't for the life of me see why.

I made my way back to Danny. He said, "Okay, Mac. What do you think?"

"Hell, Gerry, I think if you let me get down there with my Carl Gustav, then you split the boys in two lots, one team in the front door and one in the back, and when you're in position, I'll pop his 4x4s to create a diversion. Then you boys go in the front and the back at the same time. You'll find Brady with his dick in his hand, full of booze and drugs and partying just as hard as he can with two buck naked Colleens."

"No, come on, Mac. As easy as that?"

"Yeah, Gerry, I only saw the three of them and they were all just as high as they could get."

Gerry laughed and said, "These so-called hard men are entirely too confident for their own good. Okay, Mac, you lead off, I'll leave one man with our vehicles, then you create your diversion. We'll hit the front and back doors at the same time and rock this asshole's world."

When I made my way into position I could see when Gerry was in position and ready to go. When he gave me the okay, I lined my old faithful flash bang up on the first 4x4 and let fly. There was a whoosh and a thump and my target flipped over and was engulfed in an orange flash. I had just ruined Brady's party, big time. Then I did it again to his second vehicle, just to make sure he got the point.

The bits and pieces of flying vehicle hardly had time to settle when Gerry and the boys came out with Brady trussed up like a Christmas turkey, mad enough to spit nails and swearing like a Liverpool docker.

I said, "Watch his girlfriends, Gerry. They would like nothing better than to put a bullet up your ass!"

Sure enough one of them staggered out of the house with an AK47 in her hands. Luckily, she was so high that when she tried to fire a burst at us, the weapon rose up and she ended up on her ass in the rosebushes and one of the boys had no trouble disarming her. We got to go to all the best parties.

We bundled Brady into the back of a Land Rover, still trussed up and fuming. His two naked and drunken girlfriends were pushed back into the house, a job for which there was no shortage of volunteers.

On the trip to McGilligan we had to stop and put a gag on Brady as we were all heartily sick of listening to his bullshit.

When we finally arrived and made our way to the lock-up, the boys had been working so hard all the cells were full and we had to deposit our friend in a hastily erected barbed-wire compound full of similarly pissed off IRA men.

Our charge's feet did not touch the ground as we hustled him sharply from the Land Rover to the compound, divesting him of his plasticuffs and his gag on the way, and he landed on his face inside the compound.

If any of them were expecting soft treatment after what had happened, they were shit out of luck in that department.

On our way back to the wagon we came across Webber.

"Good job, lads. Get yourselves a meal and an hour's rest then we'll give you another one to pick up."

"Shit!" said Gerry as we made our way to the cookhouse. "He wasn't kidding when he said there would be no let up on this one until we caught the bastards responsible for the death of our intelligence man. But then I can't see anyone complaining about the hours we are doing on this one."

To this he got complete agreement from all of us.

An hour after we'd had our meal, we were out on the road again. This was going to be the busiest few days of our lives.

By sun-up we had collared two more of the bad boys and threw them in the compound at McGilligan. It was a case of, could they hold out as long as we could pile on the pressure? We could always call in more men, they only had a limited amount.

Also, we could have a meal and a rest break, they could not. They were kept awake around the clock. It was amazing what a little sleep deprivation could achieve. And if anyone tries to tell you it's not used anymore, don't believe them. This round-the-clock pressure was sure to show the results we were after.

I was in the cookhouse with Gerry and our crew, we were having breakfast and looking forward to an hour's cat-nap, when the duty radio operator came running in.

He shouted, "Gerry, you and Mac are wanted in the company office on the double. The large one is getting excited!"

"Hell, Gerry," I laughed. "It looks like things could be breaking!"

When we got to the office, Webber was striding about issuing orders on the radio and giving someone a good reaming!

"Mac, Gerry, we're finally getting somewhere. I knew these bastards couldn't stand this pressure for long. Your friend Brady has given us some names. He'll turn supergrass for us and testify in court, for certain concessions."

"That pig!" I burst out. "What concessions?"

Webber said, "He wants to be put into the witness protection program. He wants the full works: a new identity and a new life in Australia, along with a fat bank account. I couldn't help myself, the toys well and truly went flying out of the pram."

"They are actually considering giving that pig money and a place in Australia?"

"Calm down, Mac. He's fingering the Driscoll brothers for us, Sammy, Dave and Archie. He says they carried out the execution on the orders of the Army Council. We need to get them into court and then into the Maze Prison after a high-profile trial, just to make sure they realise what will happen to them if they mess with our undercover men again."

I said, "Bugger the prison, just give them a bullet."

"No, we need to make a well-publicised example of them with a long prison sentence at the end of it. But maybe we can organise another holiday for you with your smelly friends in the street, Mac. Before Brady makes it to Australia to spend his money. You know how good the IRA intelligence is, they might well get wind of where he is."

I said, "Why don't we just let them do the job for us, sir?"

There was no need for an explanation as Gerry was well aware of my time undercover in the streets of Derry looking for the IRA low-life that had killed my brother in the streets of Seattle.

"Right," said Webber. "I want your team babysitting Brady till we get him to court. If the IRA get anywhere near him before the trial, his life won't be worth a plug nickel, as you would say, Mac. A situation that we would welcome after the trial, but not before."

"Oh, come on, sir. Don't lumber us with a babysitting detail looking after that pig. Let us have the Driscolls."

"No, you've got your orders. Parker wants your crew on this, including you, Mac."

"Come on, Mac," said Gerry. "You know it's no good arguing. We've got the detail so we might as well get on with it and make the best of a bad job."

We collected the rest of the boys and Gerry proceeded with his briefing. The rest of the guys were not happy with our job but they soon settled down and got stuck into it.

The first question was where we were going to keep this low life.

Gerry said, "Any suggestions, Mac?"

"Yeah, I have, Gerry. Where is the one place in the Province that the IRA tried to get into more than once, but never succeeded?"

I saw Gerry's face light up. "Of course!" he said. "Right where we are now?"

"Yeah, there's an empty barrack block up the top end of the camp. Let's get the pioneers to sling a partition and a door across so we can at least lock him in and we won't have to look at him or listen to his bitching."

"Oh God, amen to that," said Gerry, remembering the trip from Derry.

When we were settled in all cosy with an around-the-clock guard on the pig Brady, Gerry went off to report to Webber.

When he came back, I said, "How long have we got to look after this pig?"

He said, "About three weeks. They're going to rush this one through. We will split the section into two groups for meal breaks so that we've got someone here with the pig at all times. I'll take one half section and you take the other, Mac. So we'll have to prepare ourselves for a long and boring three weeks with this asshole. If they're going to have a go, it will happen when we move him to the trial."

And so it went, one boring week stretched into another, and by the end of the three weeks we were all so pissed off with our guest that we would have happily done the job for the IRA!"

Webber came around and assured us that the Driscoll brothers were safely in custody. As long as we got Brady safely to court to testify, this job would soon be over. And the sooner the better for all of us.

One day Webber came barrelling into our cosy little lock-up.

"Good news, guys," he shouted. Webber never did anything quietly if he could help it. "Right," he carried on, just as loud. "They've set up a temporary court at Ballymoney Airport. We'll move Brady there by helicopter tomorrow and they'll bring the Driscoll brothers down from Belfast. The whole trial will be conducted in the secure area at the airport and we won't have to leave the airport for the duration of the trial. We'll be responsible for security, of course, but it won't be a problem as we'll be within the area of the base at all times. Have your boy ready to move by 0800 hours."

Webber turned to Parker. "Anything you need to add, sir?"

"Yes," said Parker. "When we move him tomorrow, we'll use three Wessex helicopters. Anyone waiting outside to take a shot will have to play the shell game – three identical helicopters, all leaving at the same time. Hopefully they won't waste an RPG, unless they know which one to shoot at. It is most important that you get Brady safely to that trial. It will all fall to pieces without him."

"Jesus, Mac," sighed Gerry as we left the briefing to return to our babysitting job. "This pig Brady is going to get a swelled head from all this attention. He'll be full right up with his own importance."

"Yeah," I had to agree. "But only till after the trial, then he'll be fair game again."

The next morning, after breakfast, we were assembled on the edge of the football field waiting for the choppers. We carried enough weapons and ammunition to make any attempt by the IRA to take Brady away from us a very expensive proposition on their part.

Finally, we heard the roar of the three giant noise-makers coming in.

Brady kept up a steady flow of questions.

"What's happening? Where are we going? Do you realise how important I am?"

He went on and on until we were all heartily sick of his voice.

Finally, I grabbed him and threw him into a seat as we boarded the chopper.

I said, "Listen to me, Brady. Either you sit in that corner and shut your mouth, or we will turn you loose in the streets of Derry and let the local Army Council boys know who has been shooting his mouth off!"

He suddenly went very silent and turned a very sickly shade of green.

Of course, there was no way we could turn him loose, but just the thought of what would happen was enough to scare the living shit out of him and silence him.

The three choppers took off simultaneously; the first and the third branching off in other directions while we set a course for Ballymoney Airport.

The journey by chopper was much quicker and safer than by road. With a road convoy, the bad boys could just plant a roadside bomb and then it was just a case of waiting for an army vehicle to drive by and then hitting the remote control.

But we couldn't get complacent just because we were in the air. Although much rarer, there were still attacks on helicopters, but unless they were waiting for a specific flight, they tended to save the RPGs and much rarer stingers for a sure thing, and we were hoping that with all this secrecy, that it wouldn't be us. But just in case, we had two men sitting in the doorway secured by safety harnesses and holding GPMGs.

I sat behind the one on the left and Gerry the one on the right. We were there to spot for them and feed them with ammunition.

We were about 15 minutes into the up till then uneventful journey when I spotted a line of tracer fire creeping up from an open-backed 4x4 parked on the side of the road.

I slapped the gunner on the shoulder and pointed out the deadly firework display creeping ever closer, reaching out for our chopper.

I saw our tracers slam into the open 4x4, just as our pilot threw the chopper over into a tight 180-degree turn to get away from the deadly stream of lead reaching out for us.

Then our pilot slammed the machine over and dropped steeply down onto the runway, still avoiding the deadly stream of fire still clawing for us. Luckily, we were all strapped in and we didn't have anyone flying out the door during his violent aerial gymnastics. We had a bit of a rough ride, but no one was injured. The only casualty was a few bullet holes in our trusty eggbeater.

We would probably never know if someone had just waited near the airport for a lucky strike on the off chance, or if we had a breach of security.

An RAF three-tonner pulled up beside our chopper and we threw one very frightened witness in the back none too gently, covered in his own vomit, smelling of urine and shaking like a leaf, but strangely silent now, finished complaining for the time being.

The three-tonner deposited us in front of a small self-contained accommodation block, which was to be our home for the duration of the trial.

As the boys were bundling Brady into our five-star accommodation, and that wasn't a joke. Compared to our beloved Sailor's Rest, the RAF did indeed enjoy five-star accommodation on all their bases. Just then, an RAF flight sergeant pulled up in a pretty blue Land Rover with the famous Roundels painted on the side, jumped out looking for whoever was in charge, and I pointed him in Gerry's direction.

As it turned out, he only wanted to inform Gerry that our meals would be delivered along with anything else we required. We were informed that all base personnel would be kept away from us at all times. No one was allowed to have anything to do with Brady until after the trial, except for us.

Then Webber made an appearance, bellowing loud enough to be heard all over the base.

"Mac! Gerry!" shouted the dulcet-toned one.

The boys had settled Brady in, pointing him towards the showers, which he emerged from decked out in British Army denims. That reminded me of the yearly progress reports filed by the senior officers on our performance. The standing joke was, "This man is a good soldier who works well in denims under supervision".

"Right," said Webber. "The trial starts tomorrow. The Driscoll brothers are here in the air force lock-up and there is a full platoon guarding them around the clock, even the base commander can't get near them. When the court is ready for your man, you will deliver him and then stand guard around the makeshift courthouse till they are finished with him. Then you'll bring him back here till they want him again. That's all you've got to do. Every day until the end of the trial. But don't get complacent, the IRA would love to get someone in here to do for Brady and this whole circus is for nothing if they succeed. Not an easy job for them, I know, given where we are, but not an impossible one. They've only got to sneak a bomb in here with a civilian worker and that will be the end of the story, and probably a good few of us as well.

"Gerry, I want you to split your men into two lots. You'll be in charge of one half section and Mac the other.

One of you will be awake and on duty 24/7. Any questions?"

"Yeah," said Gerry. "Any chance of a few more bodies around here?"

"I'll see what I can do," said Webber. "Don't forget, if you lot fuck up, this whole thing will fall apart in quick time!"

"Don't worry, sir. Mac and I will handle it."

"Good," said Webber. "I'll see if I can find you a couple of extra bodies," then he was gone.

And so we established our routine, even before the trial had started. We had someone in with Brady at all times and either Gerry or I were around at all times.

It was two days before we got the call to bring the pig down to the makeshift court. We used three Land Rovers, one in front with two men on board to run interference, one in the middle with me driving and Brady in the back with two men, and another two men bringing up the rear. Like Gerry said before, this pig was going to get delusions of grandeur before we were finished, but we had been told not to get complacent and we wouldn't.

The first time he was only in there an hour. I don't know what was going on in there but that wasn't my problem, my problem was to make sure no unauthorised personnel got in there while I was in charge of security outside.

He had been inside only about 20 minutes when the base commander decided to check out my security. Group Captain Smythe Jameson was the very epitome of posh and a long-service man with a low opinion green army grunts. He got out of his chauffer-driven car and sauntered to the door.

I saluted him smartly and said, "Good morning, sir."

"Good morning, Private," and his haughty voice told me straight away that he thought he was talking to something he scraped from the bottom of his shoe.

He said, "I'm just going in to check on proceedings in there."

I stood firmly in his way and said, "Sorry, sir. My orders are that no one goes in there until my witness is finished and I return him to his secure accommodation!"

He said, "Do you know who I am?" in that oh so upper-crust voice.

I said, "Yes, sir. I know who you are, but as I said, those are my orders."

He shouted for his driver, "Flight Sergeant Weller, this American person is trying to stop me from going in there. Please remove him!"

I could tell by the look on Sergeant Weller's face that he knew the score, but now he had to explain to his commander the folly of his ways, and he didn't seem to be looking forward to the job at hand. Just then, a very large private called Sammy Jones appeared at his side carrying an SLR and looking like he was comfortable with using it.

"Any problems, Mac?" he asked quietly.

"No, I don't think so, Sammy. These gents are just leaving!"

The unhappy looking flight sergeant lead his spluttering commander back to his car and the ever-so-posh officer was still throwing threats over his shoulder as he got into the back seat.

"This is not over, Private!"

I said, "Yes, sir. Of course, sir," and saluted him smartly once again!

When they escorted Brady back out of the court and into my care again, Webber collared me as they were back into the wagon.

Webber said, "Have you been upsetting the local fly boys, Mac?"

"Who me, sir?" I said innocently. "I was only explaining my orders to them, sir."

The large one chuckled and said, "Good job, Yank. Good job. But there is no need to show off."

I snapped smartly to attention and said, "Yes, sir. Of course, sir. Leave to carry on with my duties, sir!"

The large one let out a strangled laugh and said, "Fuck off, you old Yankee bastard!"

We moved Brady the pig back to our digs and got him settled in. The next job was for Gerry to go down to the cookhouse and supervise the loading of our evening meal, into the good old-fashioned hay boxes used by all branches of the services to deliver hot meals to the men in the field. And with Gerry he could pick out our food at random from all over the kitchen, making it harder for an IRA sympathiser from the civilian workers to slip poison into Brady's food; to succeed at that they would have to poison the whole base.

We carried on with our routine day after day, seeing to the security of the court when Brady was attending, then the round-the-clock security of our digs and supervising our meals. All the while wondering where and when the bad boys would hit us.

They didn't have the manpower, or the weapons to hit us with a frontal assault. They had tried that before at McGilligan when they had weapons and reinforcements from a North African despot, but that little excursion ended very badly for Irish and North African alike.

Which only left them two options: they could not come in by air as this would bring them smack up against the famous RAF regiment. So they had a choice of a mortar attack, and their experience with mortar attacks had proven to be notoriously inaccurate in the past, or they could send a bomb in with civilian workers who had access to the base.

As it happened, the Army Council realised what they were up against and decided to cut their losses. They decided to sacrifice the Driscoll brothers. A week went by without incident. The Driscolls were convicted and packed off to the Maze Prison in Belfast in a blaze of publicity to spend many years incarcerated there.

Hopefully the IRA would now realise they couldn't mess with our undercover men in the streets and our intelligence would continue to flow.

As for Brady, the Sons of Erin had very long memories and he wouldn't be safe for a very long time, no matter what country they moved him to.

Ten days later another longhair turned up at The Rest and spent an hour in the office with Parker and Webber.

After he left we were called into the conference room and Parker got straight to the point.

"Right, that was Colonel Samson, he's in charge of 14 Company. He wanted to extend the thanks of his men and himself for our part in the quick capture and conviction of the killers of Captain Stephens. He is sure our efforts will go a long way towards making their time in the Province much safer. Thank you."

When he went back to his office, Webber said, "Okay, you lot. This isn't a holiday camp, back to work! Check the duty roster."

Back to the old routine.

Chapter Seventeen

Ram Raiders

The idea of stealing a JCB and ramming it into a bank to tear out the cash dispensing machines to get to the cash inside is not a new idea.

The IRA were heavily into this practice when they needed to top up their cash boxes, so they could buy arms, ammunition and explosives.

But with the expert intelligence gathering of 14 Company, they quite often found the SAS waiting for them with a nasty surprise when they broke into the bank.

For a while there were scoreboards in every military establishment in the Province, reading SAS – 3, IRA – nil, and so forth. As another raid was foiled, so the score would increase as the campaign went on.

Normally these raids would be handled by the regiment, until one day at The Rest we had a visit from a 14 Company long-hair, as we called them. In their highly dangerous line of work, they had to look as unmilitary as possible. Long hair, straggly beards and tatty dirty clothing were the order of the day.

This particular long-hair was closeted in the office with Parker and Webber. The Rest was abuzz with rumours. We all knew who this guy was and a visit from a 14 Company spook was unprecedented.

Eventually the company clerk came around with a list of names. Sergeant Gerry Anderson, Corporal Dave Edwards, and six privates were on the list and I was one of them.

"Right," said Smithy, the company clerk. "Everyone on that list is to report to the conference room in one hour."

Danny said, "What do you think, Mac? This is something else."

I said, "I guess we'll find out in an hour, Sarge."

Danny laughed. "Shit, Yank. If you were any further laid back you'd fall over. Don't you ever get worked up about anything?"

"Come on, Danny. There's no point in worrying about it, we'll find out in a bit," I laughed.

Finally we were all gathered in the conference room and waiting, when Parker, Webber and the spook wandered in.

Parker started the ball rolling and said, "Right, guys. This is Captain Franklin from 14 Company and he's here to give us a briefing."

Franklin stood up and prepared to give us the good news, and we all knew it was going to be big or 14 Company wouldn't be here in the first place. When he started off he had all our attention.

"Okay. I'll get right to the point. You all know about the spate of bank raids we've been having in the Province. We've had intel that the IRA are going to hit the local Allied Irish Bank here in the town square. We know when they plan to do it and we want you guys to be waiting there when they break in to give them the surprise of their lives!"

Danny piped up. "What about the Regiment? They usually handle these jobs."

Franklin said, "The Regiment boys are fully committed at a bank in Belfast and one in Coleraine. I suppose the Army Council thought that if they spread themselves out enough we wouldn't be able to cover everything, so the brass made the decision to involve you guys here," he said. "The plan is to get you guys into the bank in the early hours of the morning. You'll have ten days to start a growth of beard. We'll have to cover your hair with hats and I'm sure we can find some scruffy clothes to try and make guys look un- soldierly," he grinned. "Of course, weapons will be carried under coats, so there will be no SLRs, Sterlings or Brownings. High-power pistols will be in order."

I looked at Parker, then Franklin.

"Can I make a suggestion, sir?"

"Of course, Mac," said Parker.

Franklin said, "What's your name, soldier?"

"Mallory," I said.

"Right, Private Mallory. What have you got?"

"Well, sir. The local police station is only three doors down from the bank, so if we were to be brought in as prisoners during the day, we could make our way over the rooftops after dark and down into the bank!"

Franklin smiled. "Major Parker, I like the way this man thinks. If you ever want a transfer, Yank, you just let me know, right?" he said. "So that's decided. We bring you in, handcuffed, in police vans. That way we can have your weapons waiting for you in the police station and you will be able to move into the bank in the early hours, and there isn't much chance of you being seen going over the rooftops. Any other suggestions?"

No one had anything to say, they were all so pumped. We had just been handed a plum regiment job. Shit, this was unprecedented! Franklin promised us further sit-reps as the week went by, then he and Parker left us with the large sergeant major.

"Well," he growled, "this is a turn up for the books. I don't have to tell you how important it is for us to pull this one off without a hitch! The brass want to see how we do on this. This is the first time the regiment has passed on a job like this to us, so we need to be on top of it! Also, when the hard men break into that bank, they won't be fucking around. If we are not up to it, someone is going to die. It's as simple as that. And I want to be damn sure the only ones to die are Black Balaclava Boys. You won't get a second chance. They will come in shooting and you will need to be ready to shoot back. This is not going to be just some street riot.

"Right back to your duties. We will have more intel as it comes in. And don't forget, no shaving and find the tattiest civvies possible. We will have to look the part when we go in."

We went through the following week doing the normal everyday duties: foot patrols, mobile patrols, all the normal boring everyday stuff. Franklin came back twice with intel updates. The raid was still on and we were going to be dealing with some of the worst of the local bad boys. Mickey Devlin, wanted for the murder of an RUC man; Shamus Riley killed a soldier in Belfast; Danny Collins, wanted for a bombing in Coleraine. Like Webber said, these guys weren't going to mess about; we had to be ready for anything when they came in.

Finally Saturday night came around. This was the night we would move into the bank. We were all unshaven and scruffy, most unmilitary, but then that was the idea. We didn't want to look like soldiers anyway. We had all been to the cookhouse for a meal; an army operates on its stomach, after all.

After the meal we all drew weapons and ammunition, then gathered in the conference room. We drew SMGs and Browning pistols, one grenade and one flash bang to disorientate them, and Webber shouted for me to draw the Carl Gustav out, my own flash bang that packed a serious wallop, just in case we needed to disable a JCB in a hurry. All of our weapons would be waiting in the police station when we were brought in as "prisoners".

"We've decided to have mobile patrols in the area, although not close enough to compromise you. But as soon as the balloon goes up, they will race to your position to cut off all avenues of escape."

Then Franklin piped up with, "We are expecting a six-man team with two JCBs so do not expect a walkover. They'll be heavily armed and they won't hesitate to use them."

Parker said, "We'll be monitoring you at all times from the radio room. Good luck."

Then Franklin and Parker left us in the capable hands of the big shit. Webber looked strange, unshaven and dressed in dirty jeans and an old reefer jacket.

He said, "Okay, you guys." I think my American accent and slang was finally beginning to rub off on him. "We've got to get out of here and into a covered three-tonner without anyone seeing us. So to that end Parker will throw a roadblock across each end of this road. When we know that no one is coming, we'll all nip out and get in the three-tonner and once we are all under canvas, they'll take us to Ballymoney Airport. Then we will transfer to RUC Land Rovers and we'll be taken to the local nick as prisoners. Once we are inside in the cells, our weapons will be waiting for us. Then in the early hours of the morning, Danny and his team will make their way over the rooftops and down into the bank. Mac and one other will go further down to the end of the square. Mac, I want you to take your Carl Gustav as well as your personal weapons. When the JCBs turn in and ram the bank, it will be your job to disable them. Then the mobile patrols will block their escape vehicles. Then it's just a case of mopping up. Just as easy as that.

"Right. Standby to transfer to the three-tonner."

We all moved to the front door and waited for the go ahead.

Parker was in the radio room monitoring the progress of the operation. Finally, the roadblocks were in position and he gave us the go ahead.

"Okay, Sergeant Major, get your team loaded."

Then we all nipped out and jumped in the back of the truck and the canvas covers were drawn over the back.

Then we were on the road to the airport. I curled up in the corner and closed my eyes, as usual. This prompted Danny to pipe up, "Shit. Here we go. Mac's gone to sleep again!"

Probably half an hour later we pulled up, then we were all alert again, even me. We could hear the gate guards checking us in and it was just a case of waiting patiently and we were soon shown through the gates. A couple of minutes later we pulled up again and when we piled out of the three-tonner and found ourselves behind some hangers alongside the RUC Land Rovers.

As we were being turned into prisoners, having the plasticuffs applied, I suddenly had a disturbing thought. If these RUC guys were bad-uns, then we were well and truly in the shit. But we were lucky.

After we were loaded into the back of the Land Rovers and spent another half-hour-long journey, we suddenly pulled up again at the end of our journey. Luckily for us, when we were unloaded we were in the yard of the local nick just down the road from The Rest.

We were escorted into the cells, but we were not locked in. Soon, a big burly sergeant came around.

"Okay, guys. Your weapons are here. Who's Mac?"

I put my hand up. "Yeah, that's me."

"Right," he smiled. "As well as your personal weapons, I also have an anti-tank weapon for you. I suppose you're going to stop the JCBs."

"That I am," I smiled.

"Right, all you have to do now is wait till 0200, which is when you move into position."

As it was only 2100 hours, I knew just what to do to pass the time. I went into the nearest cell and stretched out on the bunk.

As I lay down, I heard Danny pipe up, "Look out, guys. Mac's about to assume position. Somebody wake him up when it's time to move out."

Hell I was getting a reputation for being a lazy bastard, I don't know where they would get such an idea. Anyway, that was the last thing I heard till Danny shook me awake.

"Come on, Mac. Wake up, it's time to do some work."

We gathered in the station office. Everyone was keen and pumped up for what was to come.

I collected an SMG, a Browning pistol and my trusty flash bang, the Carl Gustav.

Webber said, "Can you and Corporal Edwards move out first, as you've got further to go? We'll follow on to the bank when we get the signal that you're in position."

As our old Pioneer radios were so easy to monitor – shit, all you had to do was turn your television onto BBC2 and you could pick up our voice transmissions – all I would do was give three blips on the radio Prestel, and that would be their signal that we were in place.

Dave and I moved up onto the roof and found it was easy to move along the length of the square, moving from rooftop to rooftop. It was actually a cat burglar's paradise. We moved along at a good pace and we were soon past the bank and moving on to the end of the square.

Once we were settled into the position, with a good view down to the front of the bank, I gave the three blips on the radio Prestel to tell them we were in position. Then Webber and Danny could move into position inside the bank.

I unlimbered the Carl Gustav and we got two HE rounds ready to go when things went noisy. I would only have time for two rounds to disable the JCBs then things would degenerate into a down and dirty firefight, which was where our boys excelled, and the Black Balaclava Boys were no slouches either.

Then we settled into position for the waiting game. A soldier's life was made up of 90% mind-numbing, boring waiting, followed by the sudden explosion of adrenalin-filled madness that could easily get you killed if you couldn't suddenly adjust from the boring to the madness in a split second and hit the ground running.

I settled into counting stars, studying the beauty of the clear night sky. This really wasn't the time to go to sleep again.

While I was contemplating the universe and wondering what was out there, Dave was watching the road below us, and waiting for something to happen.

As I was navigating my way around The North Star for the third time, Dave suddenly nudged me.

"I can hear engines. I think they're coming!"

Right, here we go, I thought, time to go to work. I got up on my knees with the Carl Gustav on my shoulder and Dave loaded me with the first HE round. They were coming in from both ends of the square.

I hoped our mobile patrols were on the ball because I could disable the two JCBs then they would have to box in the escape vehicles.

The first JCB raced into the square and turned into the bank with a crash. Straight away I lined up on it and put a round into the engine. The familiar whoosh followed by the orange flash and the rumbling explosion was just dying away when the second JCB crashed into the bank alongside it and Dave finished reloading me so I didn't give him a chance to reverse out and get away. I put the second round once again into the engine and the orange flash and the rumbling explosion told me the second JCB wasn't going anywhere! Now it would degenerate into that firefight!

The mobile patrols moved in straight away, blocking off the escape route of their getaway vehicles. The crackle of small arms' fire echoed around the square as the boys in the bank, under the able direction of Webber and Danny, took the fight out into the street and to the Black Balaclava Boys.

Dave and I were rushing down the back from the roof we had occupied, trying to get into the fight before it came to an end.

The mobile patrols were stopping any escapes and the boys from the bank were in the process of mopping up.

The police station had reopened to take in anyone we arrested to the cells, but at that moment we were not thinking of arrests. We were only thinking of stopping them. After all, this was our first regiment job and we were not going to screw this one up. We wanted them to say we passed a job on to those boys and they did us proud.

As we came out into the square again, we followed our mobile patrols in, rounding up anyone who tried to get past us and escape. The crackle of small arms' fire told us that they were not going to give up easily, but that was their choice. We had achieved our main goal of stopping the bank raid and now it really was a case of clearing up. But they hadn't given up yet, a firefight was going on in earnest now.

Our mobile patrols were mounted in pigs, so Dave and I joined the section from the pig, advancing behind the protective bulk of the rolling cast-iron barricade.

It was really only a matter of time now, as they were boxed in, but this was not the time to get complacent and catch one of the stray bullets flying around.

Suddenly a ricochet bounced off the pig we were following and made a mess of Dave's shoulder, and he went down with a gasp.

Luckily, the section from the pig had a medic with them and he immediately went to help Dave.

"Don't worry, Mac. Carry on, he'll be all right."

As we advanced behind the pig, I could see that the would-be bank robbers were getting the idea now and starting to surrender. They were dropping their weapons in the street, and putting their hands on their heads. Our boys and the RUC were cuffing them and taking them to the cells.

When we got the final count, we had four prisoners, including Mickey Devlin and Shamus Riley, two of the most wanted men in the Province, and two dead men, both had been driving the JCBs. The only casualty on our side was Dave Edwards and his smashed shoulder. Things could have well been a lot worse.

When things had settled down, Webber said, "What happened to Dave, Mac?"

"Just bad luck really, sir. We were following up the patrol section from the pig when he caught the ricochet from the pig itself."

"Shit!" he said. "That really was blind bad luck. Anyway, 14 Company and the regiment were impressed with our performance. So much so that we should be getting another call, and they tell me that the score will now read IRA – still nil."

Chapter Eighteen

Roadblock on the Bridge

It was a beautiful sunny Saturday morning in Derry. Bright sunlight streaming in the windows of The Sailor's Rest nearly made the old city look normal. But it was deceiving, when we got outside it was really the same cold dirty city and we still had to face the bombs and the bullets.

"Cheer up, Mac," chuckled Webber as we headed for my Land Rover to get ready for the quick trip to the Craigavon Bridge to check on the roadblocks stationed there doing the boring and mundane job of vehicle searches on the bridge. That was normally boring and mundane, but as we had seen time and time again that could all change in an explosive terrifying matter of seconds.

But the big sergeant major was in a good mood.

"Cheer up, Mac, you old Yankee bastard. Only one more week and we're out of this shit-hole and on our way back to Blighty."

I said, "Yeah, Sergeant Major, but you know this place, a lot can happen in a week and it usually does."

"Shit, Yank, you're just getting old," he laughed.

We pulled up at the road block on the top level of the bridge where Sergeant Delaney, Corporal Dennis and three privates were manning the vehicle checkpoint.

"Quiet day, Delaney?" rumbled the big sergeant major.

"Yes, sir," said Delaney. "No action at all."

But it wasn't going to stay that way for long. Just then the private on point waved in an old rusty blue Transit van for a vehicle search. We could only see two men in the front and there was no telling what was in the back. After a quiet, uneventful morning, everyone was going about the job in a relaxed manner. This was not a good idea here, it was asking for trouble, and Webber didn't like it one little bit. He started forward for the Transit to give the boys a rocket and get them on their toes. Now, we had a lot of firepower there at the time; Delaney and his boys all had SLRs and there was a GPMG up on the sandbag wall covering the queue of vehicles on the bridge road. Webber and I were both carrying Sterlings so as I said, a lot of firepower. Only a nut would want to brace us.

Unfortunately, as it turned out, that's exactly what these guys were. Just that, and though we didn't know it yet, they were carrying a load of plastique in the back of the van.

As Webber stepped up to the van, the donut in the passenger seat lifted a pistol and fired at Webber. The big guy went down in a heap in the road after the bullet had taken half his jaw away. Now in a case like that, you don't stop to ask questions and Webber, after all, was our sergeant major.

The next 30 seconds saw the van turned into a sieve as it absorbed round after round of 7.62 from the SLRs and the Jimpey and a 30-round mag of 9mm from my Sterling.

Next thing, Delaney was shouting cease fire, cease fire, and the two guys in the old Transit van were riddled. Delaney took two guys to check out the van and see to our sergeant major, while we covered the other cars on the bridge to make sure the guys in the van didn't have any back-up.

The ambulance came to pick up Webber and take him to hospital and we stayed behind to clear up the mess, something we were getting used to. The recovery wagon came for the Transit van, the meat wagon took away the two bodies and bomb disposal cleared up the load of plastic explosive, something that was getting to be routine. But this time we were short our sergeant major, something that definitely was *not* routine. Then I drove back to The Sailor's Rest in an empty and unusually quiet Land Rover, without the big guy shouting his mouth off.

I parked up in The Sailor's Rest car park and went inside. It was not the usual shouting and hollering and brash good humour, something was definitely missing without Webber; the big, brash sergeant major was definitely leaving a big hole in our lives.

Delaney came to find me, without all the noise and the "Hello, Mac, you old Yankee bastard," the whole place was quiet.

He said, "It's all right, Mac, he made it. Webber has already been flown back to England. He'll be in hospital for a while, but he'll be all right."

That was the longest speech I had ever heard from him.

I said, "Are you sure? Is he really going to be all right?"

"Yeah," he said. "The old bastard will live, but he's going home with a good part of his left cheek missing. He'll look a bit like Frankenstein's monster, but then he was always an ugly old bastard anyway."

This was another example of the soldier's morbid sense of humour. We all loved the bad-tempered old bastard, he was one of ours, ugly or not. He would be going home a week early with half his face missing but at least he was going home alive and not in a body bag.

Chapter Nineteen

Another One That Got Away

My whole being was pain, all-encompassing pain. There was a roaring in my ears as my hearing started to return. I could see nothing but a deep red haze and I could feel nothing but pain.

The pain was everything, I couldn't open my eyes, but my hearing was gradually returning and I could hear a background babble from people around me, although I still couldn't distinguish words, it was only a red haze behind my eyelids, a mish-mash of sound, an all-enveloping sensation of pain.

There was a sensation of movement, a burble of noise, the colour red and the sensation of pain.

Slowly the feeling came back to my limbs one by one, first my arms, then my legs. The pain didn't recede but it gave me something to focus on and gradually the sensation of cold and wet also came back into focus.

I was lying at the bottom of what felt like a cold wet hole, and the sensation of wet wasn't only coming from the mud at the bottom of the hole, it was also coming from the blood seeping from three bullet wounds in my body.

I knew I was cold, I knew I was wet, I also knew I was in the most severe pain possible, but I still didn't know why, or where I was, and in a way that was the most frightening part of my situation.

Gradually, the hard Ulster accent of the people around me filtered into my consciousness. I realised I was in the Province, but I still couldn't register why I was there.

More and more my focus was coming back and I remembered I was a soldier in the British Army and I had been on a street patrol in Derry when a sudden and violent explosion had brought my patrol to sudden halt.

We had walked unwittingly into a roadside bomb as we were making our way up William Street. The bomb was set off remotely from one of the houses.

My problems didn't end with the three bullet wounds, I was also suffering from shock and concussion and even worse, I was blind from the bomb flash.

As I lay in the bottom of my cold wet hole, I could hear the hard Ulster accent all around me and I knew it would only take one of them to realise that I was still alive and the best I could expect would be a quick bullet in the brain. So I just laid there pretending to be dead.

After all, soldiers are good at lying still with their eyes shut – we called it Egyptian PT, you would call it sleeping. We would get plenty of practice after a booze-up; our way of blowing off steam when the pressure got to be too much.

In those days, they used to say the American soldier had a drug problem, while the British Soldier had a drink problem. I know which one I prefer. Even after all these years, I still can't stick needles in myself so I would make a seriously useless drug addict, no matter what the circumstances.

Anyway, to get back to the story, I was still lying in a cold wet hole, bleeding and in the most excruciating pain I have ever felt in my life.

I wanted to scream, but I couldn't let the gunmen know I was still alive or my life would come to an abrupt end. I was fading in and out of consciousness, but the Ulster accents seemed to be moving away from me. I lay still, hoping against hope that they would keep moving because I was helpless. I still couldn't see and I'd lost my SLR in the confusion after the explosion. Not that I could see to shoot anyone, but I would have felt much better with the rifle in my hands.

Gradually the voices receded, but I continued to lay still in the bottom of my cold wet hole. I was shocked, bleeding, in severe pain and I was completely helpless. I was lost, blind, in British Army uniform, in a place where British soldiers were decidedly unpopular to say the least. This was a war zone, even if the politicians could only call it a police action. I'd been in a few scary situations in my time but this had to be the scariest. It was going to take a major amount of luck to get out of this one.

As I lay in the bottom of my bomb hole, cold, wet and bleeding, the pain was enough to keep me awake, even though I was pretending to be unconscious.

As I lay there, blind, racked with pain and absolutely terrified because I was totally helpless, I wondered what the hell I was going to do to get out of this one.

I suddenly heard a soft whisper, "Lie still, soldier. I'll look after you."

Well, that scared me even more as the females of Ulster were not known for being soft, especially with British soldiers.

The first British soldier to die in the '60s was in Belfast. He was surrounded by women in the street when he was separated from his patrol. An 18-year-old boy who wouldn't fire his weapon into the crowd was held down until the gunmen came and shot him. So you can see why I wasn't reassured by the female voice.

He was only a teenager; he had not lived a life at all. But I had this soft lilting female Irish voice in my ear saying, "Lie still, soldier. Lie still and wait. I'll look after you."

Well, as scared as I was, I couldn't do anything else. I couldn't see, I couldn't find my rifle, not that I could do anything with it if I did, and to top it all, I had three bullets in me.

I said, "Who are you?"

She said, "Lie quiet and wait." I had no choice. I had to do what she said.

I lay there in my cold wet hole fading in and out of consciousness and hoping against hope that she would come back again. She was my only hope.

Time passed. I don't know how much longer it was, but suddenly she was back. I felt a gentle hand on my face and she whispered, "Are you all right? Can you move?"

I said, "I don't know till I try. I can't see. How far have we got to go?"

She said, "Not far. Try and stand up and lean on me."

I struggled to my feet, with pain lancing through my body from all directions. I felt an arm go around my shoulders and I put my arm around her waist. I struggled along falteringly.

I said, "I hope we haven't got far to go, because I'm already running out of steam."

That soft lilting voice came back in my ear, "Don't worry, soldier, it's not far now."

We staggered along and then she opened a door and we staggered through and she slammed the door behind us.

A few more steps and she lowered me onto a bed. She whispered, "You are safe now," but I was already fading out again.

Back at The Rest, Dick Shelley, who was standing in for Webber as acting sergeant major whilst he was still in hospital in England getting his face repaired, was giving Major Parker the news.

"Yes, Sergeant, what is it?"

"I'm afraid we've lost a patrol up in William Street, sir," said Shelley.

"Oh God," said Parker. "Will it never end?" He sighed and said, "All right, Sergeant, give me the butcher's bill."

Shelley said, "Well, sir, it seems they walked into an ambush with a roadside bomb that was triggered remotely. Sergeant Taylor is in hospital, the doctors said it was touch and go for a while but he'll live. Unfortunately, we lost two men and Mallory is on the missing list. We couldn't find his body."

"God, Sergeant," said Parker. "If the Provos have him, he'll be better off dead."

"Yes, sir," said Shelley. "We've got patrols out looking for him. We can only hope for the best."

The first sensation that came back to me when I came around was one of all-encompassing and excruciating pain, and the colour red. The pain was enough to make me scream, but I couldn't. I still didn't know where I was, or who was around, I just had to swallow the pain back and hope for the best.

I reached up to my eyes and felt bandages, then I ran my hands gingerly over my chest and found more bandages. Whoever she was, she was trying to look after me, although I still didn't understand why.

I was in serious need of a doctor's attention and some morphine, but I wasn't complaining. Not that it would do me any good if I did.

I was in the middle of bandit country. I couldn't see and I couldn't find my rifle, but at least I was still alive. Then I froze and my heart nearly stopped as I heard a door scrape open. Now I was truly frightened.

I would have felt better with my rifle in my hands, and my eyes working but I didn't have that luxury. And anyone who tells you they are not frightened in a situation like that is a damned liar.

I heard the door scrape shut, then footsteps coming towards my bed. I breathed a sigh of relief when I heard her whisper, "Are you awake? How do you feel?"

My voice came out rough and squeaky when I replied. "I feel like I've been run over by a truck and I could do with some serious pain killers!"

She said, "I'm sorry, but bandages are the best I can do for now."

I said, "No, don't be sorry. You are my only hope of surviving this. But why are you helping me? Just imagine what the boys will do to you if they find out about this!"

"I know," she said quietly. "But there has been so much killing here. I just couldn't stand it anymore. Now lie still while I change your bandages."

And when she started to change the bandages the pain turned once more into absolute agony.

She said, "I'm sorry I'm hurting you again, but I have to do it. You have three bullet wounds, but luckily they went right through you so there are no bullets in you. You also have four shrapnel wounds from the bomb that I have managed to stitch up." But her quiet monotone was fading as I passed out again from the pain.

Gradually the grey shadows receded again and her quiet voice gradually came back to me again. I was in a cold sweat and she was sponging me down with a damp cloth.

"Sit up," she said. "I've made you some soup. Let's try and get it down you," and she proceeded to feed me. I finally got it down and managed to keep it down without being sick, then I was absolutely knackered and I started to fade out again.

"Relax and sleep now," she said softly.

I was trying to stay awake. We had to talk about me getting back to my unit, but no matter how hard I tried, I couldn't stay awake.

Eventually the grey clouds receded again and my sense of hearing came slowly back, and with that also came the pain. But this time it was different I was hot and sweaty, I was burning up! I reached tentatively up and touched my forehead, it was hot and sweaty. I also touched the skin around the bandages she had placed on my wounds; same result, my skin was sweaty and red hot to the touch.

Now I'm no doctor, but I knew enough about first aid to know I was in trouble. My body was wracked by infection and if I didn't get massive doses of antibiotics soon, I would probably die.

I had no idea how long I had been unconscious but a slight noise registered on my brain and I started to come to the surface again. The noise I had heard was the door scraping open again, and I froze in absolute terror because I had no idea who was coming in and I was under no illusions what would happen if the Black Balaclava Boys found me before my guys did. I could face these guys in the streets with my eyes working and a gun in my hands, because we had to do it every day. But blind and without a gun I was one step away from a gibbering wreck.

Then the welcome whisper penetrated my dark world of pain, and she was back. She came closer and whispered, "I'll see to your bandages now, soldier."

I said, "I'm afraid you'll have to see to more than my bandages if you want me to live."

Then she came closer and put her hand on my overheated forehead. There was a sharp intake of breath and she whispered, "Oh God!"

I said, "If you don't get me back to my unit in the next couple of days, you'll most likely have a corpse in your cellar."

"How can I get you back to the army without the IRA knowing?" she asked. "If they find out what I've done it'll be curtains for me."

"And if you don't get me back to where they can give me medical attention," I said, "it will be curtains for me and all of this will have been for nothing. The last place I want you to end up is on their death list, but if you can't get me back, you might just as well have left me in that bomb crater in William Street." Harsh, I know, but unfortunately true.

"Because they haven't found my body, there will be patrols out everywhere looking for me, so if you can contact one of them they can chuck me in the back of a Land Rover and that will be an end to it. They can get me to hospital for treatment and hopefully it won't come back on you."

My little speech was greeted with absolute silence. I could almost hear her thoughts going around and round in her head.

If the boys ever found out what she had done, she would end up on their death list and I really didn't want that to happen. After all that had happened to me, the only reason I was still breathing was because she had pulled me out of that hole and hidden me away from the Black Balaclava Boys.

I waited with bated breath in my blind world, hoping against hope that she would make the right decision.

As I lay there in my stinking bed, and I have to admit the stink was of my own making – it was 90% fear and 10% unwashed soldier – finally she made her decision.

She said in a low whisper, "Can you walk?"

I replied, "I hope so, with your help."

"Right," she said. "Pull this on," and she proceeded to drag a smelly old coat over me. Then she said, "Wait here for me now." Well, shit, where else could I go? After all, I was still stone blind.

Eventually I heard the scrape of the door opening and she was back. She whispered, "I'm going to put you on the back seat of the car." Then she covered me with something, probably an old blanket.

I was tossed about violently in the car for what seemed a long time then we finally screeched to a halt. Then the first voice I heard had a British accent, not an Ulster accent.

"You can't stop here, madam, you'll have to move along." Then came the soft Irish accent that I had grown used to.

She said, "Take him back or he will surely die. I've done all I can for him, now you have to get him to your hospitals."

I heard the back door of the car open, then a strong Cockney accent.

"Jesus, Mac! We thought you were dead!"

"Is that you, Danny?"

It was Danny Bailey from the Mile End Road.

He said, "Yeah, it's me, Mac. Christ, what has she done to you?"

I said, "Not her, Danny. She saved my life. Let her go quick, if the boys find out what she's done, she's brown bread!" As he turned and shouted for Dick Shelley, I grabbed her arm and ran my fingers over her face, trying to memorise her features and not doing a very good job of it.

"Quick!" I said. "Get away while you can, and thanks for everything. And remember, if you ever need anything, leave a message here for me." Then just like that, she was gone.

Then just in time, Dick Shelley and Danny were there, one each side to catch me as I started to fade out again.

When I came round again it was to the dull roar inside the Wessex helicopter taking me to hospital.

The loadie must have seen me moving and he plonked a pair of earphones on me and shouted, "Here, have a chat with the pilot."

Then a cheerful voice came over the intercom, "Good morning, Private Mallory, and how is our VIP passenger today."

"Oh, I feel like I've been run over by a Mac truck. But apart from that, I'm just peachey."

"Good. Good American humour on this fine morning. I'm Flight Lieutenant Jameson. We are en route to Selly Oak Hospital in Birmingham where lots of lovely nurses are awaiting your arrival so they can spoil you rotten and ply you with strong drugs."

This guy really was like the Ian Drury song *Reasons to Be Cheerful*, but I was rapidly fading out again; the grey clouds were back.

When I came round again, I was still enveloped in the dull roar of the Wessex. I've had some wild helicopter rides in my time in the army, but this one was something else. I've been shark spotting along the coast of Cyprus; laid face down in a CASEVAC basket; hung across the struts of a Wasp helicopter, and I've been Jebel hopping in the Omani Desert where the updrafts are lethal, but this trip across the Irish Sea with my eyes bandaged, had easily to be the most disconcerting.

Although I would never jump out of a working aircraft, I have used a fast rope out of a helicopter. I'm one of those air passengers that would never leave a perfectly good aircraft until it lands, but they told me this wild ride was taking me to Selly Oak, one of the best military hospitals in England and I believed them.

But I never imagined what I would see when they finally took the bandages off my eyes at Selly Oak, after all my time spent with my benefactor, the Bogside Irish girl who took me in, dressed my wounds and saved my life and then returned me to The Sailor's Rest at great risk to her own life.

Anyway, I arrived at Selly Oak in the arms of Morpheus and loving it. You know how they say that when you can't see all your senses kick in and go into overdrive? Well, this is certainly true. As I drifted in and out of consciousness, my hearing was working overtime.

I could hear my helicopter taxi whup, whup, whupping away into the distance. I could hear the medics and the nurses chattering away. I could smell that unmistakable hospital smell all around me and then a much more interesting smell cut in.

I had spent the last six months in the company of sweaty men, the smell of machine oil on weapons and vehicles, and the distinctive smell of gunpowder.

The new smell was of perfume and women. I was definitely in the company of those nurses my cheerful pilot was talking about. Although I still couldn't see anything, and I was still floating in and out on the grey clouds, I knew I was in a hospital.

When they settled me into bed and I was comfortable, I heard the door open and a rather posh voice say, "I'm

Colonel Smedley, Private Mallory, and I will be your doctor while you are here."

He fussed and bustled about and I got the impression of a fussy old busy-body. He poked and prodded, lifted bandages here and there and after a few tut, tuts and "Oh mys", he finally came to his conclusions.

"Well, well, Private Mallory. You have been in the wars, haven't you?" I heard a stifled giggle on the other side of the room and I concluded that the nurses were well used to his performance. Then he carried on.

"You have three bullet wounds and some nasty shrapnel wounds, but nothing to be worried about, just normal everyday stuff for us." And he rambled on. "We will get the eye surgeon in here to see you in the morning, but for now, I suggest you get some rest."

As it happened, I was already fading out again and I think it was a combination of 50% sleep and 50% drugs.

I don't know how long I was out this time, but as soon as I moved, there was a waft of perfume from across the room and a soft voice said, "Welcome back, Private Mallory. I'm Lieutenant Johnston and I'm your nurse. Don't worry about Colonel Smedley, He may come across as a bit of an old woman but he really is a first class battlefield surgeon and you are in good hands. How is your pain? Can I get you anything?"

I said, "Yes, Lieutenant, I am in pain, but I've had worse, and you could get me something, a new pair of eyes wouldn't go amiss." And although I said it with what I thought was a disarming grin, there was no return laugh. I sensed an awkward moment, and said, "Sorry, that was a bit of tactless. Soldier humour. But a bit of breakfast would be nice, I'm bloody starving!"

She laughed and said, "Well, Yank, a good appetite is always a good sign here. I'll get you some food and by the way, Colonel Smith will be in this morning to remove your eye bandages and examine you. And don't worry, he's the best eye surgeon here!"

"Well, feed me first, Lieutenant. And by the way, you know how they say when you lose one sense the others are heightened?"

"Yes," she said, "that's what they say."

"Well," I said, and I couldn't keep the broad grin off my face when I said it, "they're absolutely right, Lieutenant. You smell lovely."

"Oh," she said, and I could tell by her voice that she was taken aback. "Soldiers!" she exclaimed as she disappeared out the door. But I could tell by the sound of her voice that she was smiling.

Maybe I shouldn't have been winding the lovely lieutenant up, as the British boys would say, but at the time it was my only form of entertainment while I waited for the verdict on my eyes.

"Look, I'm sorry, Lieutenant. Maybe I shouldn't have wound you up, as my British colleagues back with the battalion would say, but sometimes that's all we have to keep us going, that soldier's sense of humour."

She said, "I hope that sense of humour stays with you, Private Mallory, because Colonel Smith will be here in half an hour to remove your bandages and examine your eyes.

I said, "Jesus Lieutenant, you really know how to take the wind out of a man's sails! Will you promise me something?"

"What's that?" she said.

"Will you promise to be here when he removes the bandages?"

"Yes, I'll be here," she said softly.

I said, "One more thing, Lieutenant. What's your first name? I can't keep calling you Lieutenant, can I?"

"You should be calling me Lieutenant anyway," she said. "After all, I'm an officer and you are a private."

I said, "Oh shit. Shot down in flames. Or as we say back in Uncle Sam's backyard, crashed and burned."

As I settled back on my pillows, she said with a throaty chuckle, "My name is Maggie."

As I dozed off I said, "Thank you, Lieutenant Maggie."

I actually did doze off then, which was a bit of a surprise for me and for the medical staff, considering what was resting on the removal of those damned bandages. But then again, I was still full up to my eyeballs with morphine.

Eventually Colonel Smith bustled into the room all bright and breezy, which brought me back to the surface again.

"Well, Private Mallory, how are we this morning?" Like I said, all bright and breezy.

I said, "We are just fine and dandy, Colonel. But we are waiting for you to examine my eyes!" A bit sarcastic, which I apologised for immediately. "Sorry, Colonel, but as you can imagine, the outcome of this examination is playing heavily on my mind." Then I said, "Is Maggie here?"

Straight away she said, "Yes, Private Mallory, I'm here."

I said, "Okay, Colonel, I'm ready. Let's get on with this." I may have sounded full of piss and vinegar, but that was very far from the truth and I think everyone in the room knew it.

I felt a gentle reassuring hand on my shoulder and I knew that was Lieutenant Maggie. Then I could feel hands gently touching my eye bandages, and then I could feel scissors cutting through them. Moment of truth time was here.

He said softly, "Keep your eyes tightly closed, please."

And that's just what I did. I admit that I was rigid with fear, not knowing what the results of this procedure were going to be. As the bandages came away, my perception of the world changed from complete and utter blackness, gradually to grey.

Then he said, "Okay, Mac." Shit, I had a full Colonel calling me by my first name, surreal or what? "Okay, Mac. You can open your eyes slowly, and expect some pain when the light starts to come in."

My first impression was of a blinding white light, and he was certainly right to tell me to expect some pain. In fact, it was a whole lot of pain, but then I was kind of getting used to that! In fact, there was so much pain that I had to squeeze my eyes shut again against it.

"That's all right," he said gently. "Close your eyes again and rest awhile and when you're ready, try again."

After about ten minutes, I steeled myself for another try. Then came the white light again, but not as bad as the first time. Then slowly the painful white light changed to brilliant flashing colours, and gradually my vision returned.

I looked around, drinking in the sights as my vision grew stronger.

Lieutenant Maggie was standing at the back of the room watching anxiously as things progressed. And I must say my first impressions of her, even with my bandages on, were spot on the money, she was literally a sight for sore eyes.

Anyway, back to the business at hand. As I was taking in the other sights around me, the doctor was watching me closely.

Finally he said, "We'll let your eyes rest for a couple of days then we'll give you an eye test."

Just then I heard a deep, familiar, rumbling laugh behind me and I looked around to see Webber sitting there. One half of his face was horribly distorted from his wounds from our little battle with the Black Balaclava Boys on the Craigavon Bridge.

"Come on, you old Yankee bastard, what's with all this gold-bricking?" he laughed.

"Jesus, doc. Is this what you call shock therapy in this hospital?" I just managed before I burst out laughing. "You take my bandages off and the first thing you show me is the ugliest God damn mug in the British Army! Shit, he would give Frankenstein's monster a run for his money. How the hell do you expect me to recover from that?"

And with that the medical staff in the room all joined in the laughter and the doc said, "I don't think we are going to have to worry."

Then I had to laugh as Webber roared, "Jesus, you old Yankee bastard, why are you still alive?"

"Shit, I could say the same for you, sir," I said. "You take a .45 round in the face and here you are large as life, twice as ugly and twice as ornery."

He said, "Look, old friend. I've got to spend some time down at East Grinstead at The Guinea Pig Club, so they can make me look pretty again, and the Colonel here tells me that your wounds and your eyes will take about the same amount of time."

And to that I had to laugh, "Shit, sir, they'll run out of plastic making you look pretty again."

Then came that familiar rumbling laugh building up in his chest. I was feeling brave, I would never dare to talk to him like that in the streets, in front of the boys.

He said, "The nurses here are taking a poll to see who is the ugliest soldier between you and me. And I've been told the vote is going your way."

"Well, shit," I said. "As I'm the only foreigner here, the vote will probably be fixed against me."

He laughed and said, "It's nothing to do with your country of origin, you old bugger. Seriously, Mac, get yourself fit again by the time I'm finished at East Grinstead and we'll go back to Derry together and sort out the old company and probably save Major Parker from a heart attack."

"Or give him one, when he sees your ugly mug," I laughed. "Right, you big bastard, you're on. I'll be ready to go back before you are. I'll have Lieutenant Maggie as a personal trainer."

I was wrong, not for the first time, about the big bastard. He was there waiting when Lieutenant Maggie discharged me and said goodbye.

"Come on, you old Yankee bastard. Let's find a pub that can put up with us for a few hours and I'll bet you anything you like that you end up under the table before me!"

And I have to say, the big sod was right. I couldn't keep up with him in the field or at the bar.

Eventually we ended up on a train, with the big bugger telling me about all his plans for getting the company safely through the coming months in the streets and back to England.

But I still wonder after all these years, who the Ulster girl was that saved my life, and I still don't know if she was Catholic or Protestant. But the most important thing was that she got through it all safely. After all, she saved my life.

Chapter Twenty

The Marching Season

One of our busiest times in the Province was when they started their yearly marches. The marches might have meant something 300 years ago when they first started having them, but now they meant only one thing to us, and that was trouble with a capital T.

The Catholics would march through the Protestant areas, I'm sure it was all to wind each other up because that was always the end result, then things would reach flash point and out would come the bombs and the bullets and we would be stuck in the middle trying to keep the two factions apart.

Things could very quickly change from a peaceful march, with the bands playing and the banners flying, then deteriorate into a madness of high-velocity bullets flying in all directions, Land Rovers speeding through the streets with flames flying from them after having a petrol bomb smashed over them and explosions sounding from every direction.

And what did they gain from it all? Nothing as far as I could see. It wasn't only British Army soldiers left bleeding and dying in the streets at the end of it all; it was their own people as well. It didn't make any sense to me, but then 13-year-old boys throwing grenades into the back of passing army lorries didn't make any sense either.

Things were warming up and Webber had us all ready to go at five minutes' notice from the first sign of trouble. We were lazing about all over The Sailor's Rest, looking in complete disarray, but in fact we all had weapons and belt kits close to hand, just waiting for things to kick off.

And we all knew that things could kick off at a moment's notice. Especially as the Prods were threatening to march through the Bogside today. This was a complete Catholic stronghold and would be certain to light the blue touchpaper and the madness would begin all over again.

Webber came past as I was lounging about in the canteen with a Coke and watching the television.

"Damn, how come you're awake, you old Yankee bastard? You've usually got your eyes shut when we are not in the streets"

I was fast gaining a reputation for being able to sleep on a clothesline.

"Just chilling out and watching the news, boss. Not that I've seen any good news."

He said, "You up for this today, you old bugger? If they get anywhere near the Bogside it will be a bad one."

"Hell, you know if they get going it will be a bad one," I said. "It always is, boss."

Just then the PA system cut in.

"Number One platoon to standby! Number One platoon to standby!" it blared.

"Come on, you old bugger," roared the big shit. "You're driving me today. Let's go and have some fun."

And we all knew Webber's idea of fun had always been a bit suspect. As I said, we may have looked like we were slouching about in complete disarray but within minutes, men, weapons and ammunition were all in the vehicles waiting for the off.

As 300lbs of sergeant major landed in the front passenger seat and a corporal and two privates in the back, I said, "Right, boss. Where's it at?"

"Rosemount School," he said. "The silly bastards are after the Redcaps there."

Less than five minutes of high-speed driving – well, as high speed as you could get in an old soft-skin Green Machine anyway – with Webber shouting in my ear, "Come on, Mac! Let's give those bastards some stick!" he took us to the top of William Street just below the Rosemount School, where we ran into what seemed like a solid wall of bricks and stones.

The glass in my windscreen suddenly crazed over from a veritable rain of missiles being thrown at us and Webber bashed it out with the butt of his rifle so that I could keep going. This was definitely not the place to park up, the natives were decidedly restless and the madness had well and truly begun.

I swung my wagon in through the gates of the school without slowing and the three-tonner with Shelley and his platoon on board was hot on my heels.

The school was an old building in a walled compound, so once the Redcap sergeant who had let us in had swung the gates shut again, we were in a pretty good position. Shelley quickly got his boys sorted out all round the perimeter then all we had to do was keep the crazies out until two and three platoon could clear them away from the school. But little did we know that two and three platoon were tied up with their own problems down by the Craigavon Bridge.

Just then there was a loud whoosh and a deafening bang as one of those crazies on the other side of the road in a third floor window picked that moment to put an RPG round through the front door of the school, blowing it right off its hinges and scattering Redcaps in all directions. Things had very definitely gone noisy.

I dropped to one knee and started to put round after round of 7.62 through the offending window. Then the GPMG gunner in the back of my wagon followed suit.

After half a belt had been used, Webber called for a cease fire. We couldn't go in and clear the house in the normal way, this time we were fully committed in the school compound.

Webber shouted, "Mac, get that Carl Gustav out of your wagon and pop an HE round through that damned window. That will keep them busy till we can get someone from Two Platoon in to clear the place!"

Well, the Carl Gustav is a modern version of the old bazooka and it really was a bit of overkill for this job – it was really an anti-tank weapon. But if that was what the big bugger wanted, that was what he was going to get.

It took me no time at all to unlimber the weapon and select an HE round from the box in the back of my wagon. I made sure there was no one behind me, because the back blast from the Venturi was deadly if anyone was too close.

I laid the sights on the offending window across the road and let fly. There was a loud boom followed by a whoosh similar to the noise of the RPG. The effect when the round went through the window was devastating and the resulting explosion could have been heard all over Old Derry. All the glass and the window frame disappeared in a gout of flame and the big bugger roared with laughter.

"Good shot, Mac! I think you've well and truly cleared that room. Now let's get these Redcaps sorted!"

Inside we quickly cleared the rubble from the doorway and found two badly wounded Redcaps that needed CASEVACing to hospital for urgent treatment.

We found five more inside with cuts and bruises, who were spitting nails and itching to get stuck into the Black Balaclava Boys, so we made sure they were suitably armed and sent them out to beef up Shelley's crew on the perimeter. Then Webber called for a Wasp helicopter to CASEVAC the two badly wounded Redcaps to hospital.

He shouted, "Mac, get Shelley and his boys to watch out for snipers when the chopper comes in. These buggers would love to knock it out of the sky."

I went outside to find Shelley and pass the message on. I found him near the gate with the Redcap sergeant that had let us in.

"Oi, Sarge!" I called. "We've got a Wasp coming in to CASEVAC two of the Redcaps inside who are in a bad way and the boss says to keep an eye out for snipers. They would love to down a chopper!"

"Okay, Mac," he said. "Stay here at the gate, will you, while I go around to the boys and get them ready."

The Redcap sergeant went inside to see to his men who were off to hospital and I took over at the gate.

Across the road, the house that I had cleared of the RPG was still burning and the natives in the road were still restless and every now and again a petrol bomb would sail over the wall lighting up the courtyard for us.

Shelley came back.

"The boys are all ready for the chopper to come in. You can go back inside now if you want," he said.

"No, you're all right, Sarge, the Redcap sergeant is inside with his boys. I'll stay out here with you."

"Hell, Mac," he said. "I didn't know you cared, you old Yankee bastard."

I turned to him with a rude remark on the tip of my tongue and just then there was a loud crack and the top of his head exploded like a melon that had been dropped from a height onto a concrete floor and I was suddenly covered in brains, blood and gore. Everyone in the compound moved quickly to whatever cover they could find, and I dived down behind my Land Rover.

I didn't have to crawl over to Shelley, it only took a cursory glance to know that he was gone. Jesus, Shelley! He had been with us from the start and he was gone in a split second.

As I lay there wiping the blood and gore from my face, Webber shouted across, "How is he, Mac?"

My voice came out in a hoarse croak and I had to try twice to get it out, but finally I croaked, "No, he's gone, sir."

I heard "Oh shit" from Webber, then straight away he was on top of his game again. "Right come on, you bunch of old ladies. Let's get sorted! Mac, anyone out there see where that shot came from?"

"Not me, boss."

Just then, one of the guys piped up on the perimeter, "Yeah, I saw it, Mac. It came from next door to the house you popped with the HE from the Carl Gustav!"

"Right," shouted Webber. "Everyone stay in cover and lay down some fire on that goddamn house." And straight away two GPMGs opened up with several rifles and they poured fire into the front of the house, making a deafening racket.

The next thing I knew, a large sergeant major landed next to me and he rumbled like the big bear that he was, "Jesus, Mac, we've got to take that bugger down and we've got to do it fast. Got any ideas?"

"Only three, sir," I said. "Either I pop another round of HE in there, or we whistle up some of the other guys to clear that house, or we need to create diversion to keep that sniper busy while we nip around the back way through the alley and give him the good news that way."

"The only problem is our other guys are fully committed down by the Craigavon Bridge," he rumbled. "But we have to sort it out quick. I've had to put the chopper on hold till we clear that bugger out."

In the meantime "that bugger" continued to keep our boys pinned down with rifle fire. Webber and I were down behind my Land Rover, which I was going to be writing another long report for on the subject of bullet holes in my vehicle, yet again.

Quickly the large one made up his mind,

"Right, Mac," he growled, "I didn't want to split our little gang up because we're fully committed here, but I think we'll have to. I'm going to take three of our guys and work our way around back. I'll leave you in charge here with the Redcaps, we'll go out the side gate and when we are in position and all set, we'll give you three clicks on the radio, then you put another HE round in the front door. As soon as you do that we'll go in from the back and clear the place."

He called the Redcap sergeant over to us behind my wagon, which attracted a couple more bullet holes in my paintwork. Then he quickly outlined our plan to him and the sarge had the unenviable job of getting back across the compound to his men and letting them in on the plan.

While he was doing that, I quickly got my trusty Carl Gustav out of the back of the Land Rover with one HE, which was all I would have time for. I found if I sat at the back of the Land Rover looking round, I could make out the door that I wanted.

Webber and his three oppos were ready at the side gate and I waved to the Redcaps to start laying down fire to keep the sniper's head down. As they started pouring rounds into the door, I gave Webber the thumbs up and they slipped out the side gate as the Redcaps continued to fire and distract the sniper. I was ready with the Carl Gustav, waiting for the three clicks on the radio Prestel from Webber. It was just a case of keeping the sniper busy until he got into position and the Redcaps were enthusiastically expending round after round in his direction to do just that.

Finally I got the three clicks I was waiting for. Webber and his boys were ready and waiting. I came up from behind my Land Rover with the Carl Gustav on my shoulder, moved quickly to the wall, lined up on the front door before our sniper could take a potshot at me and let fly. The Carl Gustav was virtually recoilless thanks to the boffin that invented the Venturi. The rear end of the piece made its reassuring "boom" and flames belched out of the back end.

The resulting explosion of the front door and frame was nothing short of spectacular as it was obliterated, which brought a ragged cheer from the Redcaps, who as I said before, were spitting nails and raring to have a go at the Black Balaclava Boys in retribution for their earlier treatment of their comrades. The Redcaps ceased fire immediately because they knew our boys were on their way in from the back.

We at the front had ceased fire, but our boys coming in from the back certainly hadn't. The firing coming from inside the house was quite fierce for about 30 seconds and then there was complete silence.

Finally the front door opened and Webber appeared pushing a black clad, blackened and bleeding young man with his arms secured tightly behind his back with plasticuffs.

They crossed the road quickly, Webber dragging our sniper none too gently behind him, and one of the boys was carrying an AK47, supplied, no doubt, thanks to the "mad colonel" in Libya.

When the gate was closed behind them once more, Webber unceremoniously dumped the snivelling soldier of the revolution on the ground by my wagon.

I looked Webber in the eye and said, "I'm surprised he survived that little bundle, boss, considering what he's done."

Webber said, "Yeah, well, I wish he'd resisted a bit more, Mac, but when we got in there, we found him huddled in a corner crying his eyes out and temporarily deaf as a post from your special 'flash bang' that you treated him to just before we came in, so we had to arrest him."

"Jesus, sir, do we really want to arrest him after what he did to Dick Shelley?"

"I know how you feel, Mac. In fact, all the rest of these boys feel the same as you, but we caught him and he surrendered, so we had to arrest him. You know that!"

"Normally I don't question anything you tell me, sir. It's just that after our little shoot-up on the Craigavon Bridge when you lost half of your face to a .45 slug and they sent

153

you to East Grinstead to replace it with plastic, it was Shelley that came to me and told me that you were okay and you had been CASEVACed out. If it comes to a choice between Shelley and that black-clad bastard, you know which way we are going to vote."

"Jesus, Mac, you know this guy has surrendered and we are going to have to turn him in. Now if you are going to argue with me, and I must say it would be a first if you did, can we do it back in my office and not in front of the men?"

I said, "Look, I'm sorry, sir. You know I've never questioned your orders, or gone against you, it's just that after all the worthless bastards we've had to put away on this tour, I just think that seeing who he killed, one more wouldn't have gone amiss."

Then the big bugger dropped a bombshell on me, when he chuckled, "You know, Mac, as close as we have just come to an argument, what I have to say to you now will probably bring that argument right on. I want you to look after Shelley's platoon until I can get a replacement in."

"Come on, sir!" I exploded. "You know how I feel about promotion. You've got Corporal Smith you can give the job to!"

He said, "Yes, I could. But you know Smithy hasn't got anywhere near the experience that you have! Now can we please finish this job and carry on this argument in my office back at The Rest?"

"Okay, sir," I said. "Just as long as you know that you're still going to get an argument," and he wandered off back into the school, chuckling away, and leaving me with the cowering prisoner. Even though he knew just what I wanted to do to the cowering wretch, he also knew that I would never disobey an order from him.

Our next job was to get that chopper in and CASEVAC the two badly wounded Redcaps to hospital. I went over to Corporal Ian Smith, who was next in command to Shelley.

"Look, Ian. You should be in charge of these guys but the big guy wants me to take command. Now I know you've got the tapes—" but the boy stopped me there.

He said, "Look, Mac, the big shit's right. I have the rank but you have the experience. I'll be happy to be your second in command until they can send up a new three-striper to take over."

"Look, Ian," I said. "We'll do the job between us till that happens, but first we have to finish this job, the big shit's right about that. But let's leave it like this, you're in charge, but you can ask me for advice any time you want! Now let's get this perimeter secure so that we can get the Wasp in and CASEVAC these Redcaps to hospital. And while you're doing that, get someone to secure this black-clad bastard. I don't trust myself to be around him."

"Right, Mac, I'll see to that while you go back to the large one and get that chopper organised."

The Redcaps had put Dick Shelley in a body bag and moved him inside with the wounded. But sadly, that was as far as he was going for now, the wounded Redcaps had to take priority. Dick Shelley wasn't in a hurry now.

I went inside and found Webber on the radio organising the chopper.

"All set out there, Mac," he said.

"Yeah, boss. Smithy has the perimeter and the prisoner secured. We're all ready for the chopper."

"Stick with him, Mac, he's really green and he'll need looking after."

"We've got it sorted," I said. "Don't worry, boss, he's in charge but he can come to me for advice any time he wants."

"Good, good," rumbled the big sod. "Look after him, Mac."

I said, "Yeah, I'll get my flash bang ready. Anyone silly enough to have a go at our chopper will get one hell of a surprise!"

155

"Go for it, Mac," said the big shit. "We've lost enough on this little outing and top on the list was Dick Shelley, a 20-year man. We definitely don't want them to get a chopper as well, our street cred would never recover and you know as well as I do, in a place like this we survive on our street cred."

"Don't worry, sir. Anyone having a go at that chopper will pay dearly."

I went back outside to check on Smithy and the boys to make sure they were on the ball, but Smithy had it all organised. The boys were all stood too, and sharp as tacks.

"Smithy, I'm going to get the Carl Gustav ready. Anyone who has a go at that chopper has to go down hard and fast!"

The boy said, "Don't worry, Mac. I won't let you down."

I just hoped this kid wouldn't come unstuck like Shelley did. He was my responsibility now.

I went to the back of my wagon and made the anti-tank weapon ready. If I had to use it I would have to be quick; the pilot and his number two and the casualties would be depending on me.

Smithy gave me the thumbs up. We were all ready and waiting and that was all we could do for now.

Webber and the Redcaps were already inside when the chopper came in. We would have to be quick loading up so he could have a quick turnaround and take off again, so as not to give the restless natives time to have a pop at the chopper or the casualties.

Suddenly I heard the hover-mower buzz of the little chopper in the distance, growing louder and louder by the second. All eyes were on the sky and our immediate surroundings as the little bird came closer and closer. I had the Carl Gustav up and ready and I could see all the boys on the perimeter tensed and waiting for something to shoot at.

Our little buzzing dust-off settled into the compound and instantly two stretchers were strapped onto it and it started to lift off straight away.

Movement in a top floor window across the road suddenly caught my eye. Shit, it was a rifle barrel and it was pointed down into the compound at our little chopper. Wouldn't these silly buggers ever learn?

I couldn't wait for orders from the big sod, there wasn't time. Once again, I laid my sights on an upstairs window and there was the reassuring "boom" from the anti-tank weapon as the window and the rifle barrel disappeared in a belch of flame and a roaring explosion as the HE round smashed home.

The little Wasp buzzed away safely in the direction of the hospital, hopefully in time to save the lives of the two Redcaps strapped to the baskets underneath.

Webber came over.

"Nice shot, Mac," the big shit growled. "Shit, you would think these buggers would have learned by now that we bite back. We'll send the meat wagon later to clear up what's left of that one."

"Just one thing, sir," I said, looking him straight in the eye. "Not the one that took Shelley to the morgue. That asshole across the road is not good enough to ride with the sarge, even if the bastard is in little pieces."

Webber looked at me strangely and I said, "I'm dead serious, sir. If there isn't another wagon available, that bastard can stay there and rot."

Slowly a little smile crept over his ruined face and memories of the shoot-up on the bridge came creeping back.

He said, "You know what, Mac? I think this job is turning you into a right hard ass. Do me a favour, old friend, don't ever get pissed off with me, will you!"

And I couldn't keep the smile off my face as I busied myself cleaning the Carl Gustav and putting it to bed in the back of my wagon, all oiled and ready for the next time I needed it.

I had a quick walk around the perimeter with Smithy to check everything was secure.

"Everything seems okay here, Smithy. You got any problems?"

"No, we're fine here, Mac. You go inside with the big fellow."

I said, "Keep an eye out for the meat wagon, Smithy. They'll be moving Dick Shelley soon."

That brought a sad look to the boy's face, and he said, "Okay, Mac. We'll sort that out."

"Look, Smithy," I said. "We've got to roll with things. This shit is part of our job, and by the way, if they try to pick up the pieces of that last clown I popped in the same wagon, let me know because he does not deserve to ride in the same wagon as the sarge. We shouldn't have any more trouble tonight. I think they've run out of steam again. But keep sharp, mate, you never know."

"Okay, Mac. Don't worry, we're on top of it."

"Good lad," I said, and gave him a slap on the shoulder.

When I got inside Webber was on the radio sorting things out so I stood back and waited for him to finish. When he finished he called me over.

"Okay, Mac. How are things outside?"

"Cushy, sir," I assured him. "Smithy's on top of it. The compound is secure and he's waiting for the wagon to come for the sarge. I hope you order a separate one for that pile of crap across the street."

"Yeah, don't worry, Mac. I made it clear to them that Dick rides on his own."

Then he shook himself tiredly and forced himself to get on with the job at hand.

"Right, old friend," he rumbled. "This is how we stand. Tell Smithy to watch out for the Redcap reinforcements coming in. Also, a company of Gurkhas are coming up to secure this place for a week or so after we go, in case these idiots get any more silly ideas."

That brought a low whistle from me and I said, "You know, boss. I kind of hope they do have ago at the 'little smiley guys', they'll be in for one hell of a shock if they don't treat them with respect."

That brought a chuckle from the large one.

"Talk about stirring up a hornet's nest," he laughed.

I said, "Where to, then? Down to the bridge to help the boys out?"

"No," he said. "That's all quiet now. The brass are of the opinion that was all a diversion to draw attention away from this place."

"If it was," I said, "they certainly got their fingers burned again!"

"Yeah," he said sadly. "Trouble is, they cost us a good man this time."

"Goddamn Easter marching season," I grumbled as I went out to the compound to make sure Smithy and the boys were ready for our relief coming in. As it happened, the Redcaps and the little guys rolled in at the same time. I showed the Redcaps and the Gurkha captain into the school where our bear of a sergeant major awaited them. I had to suppress a smile when Webber saluted the little smiley guy, who was about a third of his size, if that, and I couldn't help but think what a shock the Black Balaclava Boys would get if they underestimated these little guys.

I wandered back outside to where Smithy was handing over to a Gurkha sergeant with an unpronounceable name, and an ear to ear smile across his face.

Just then the wagon showed up to collect Shelley and I showed the medics his body bag. This represented the sad end to a 20-year army career.

The med corp corporal in charge came over to me and said, "I hear there are some bodies across the road to clear as well, Yank. Can you show me where they are."

I said, "Yeah, when you get another wagon up here. They are not riding in the same wagon as the sarge."

"Hell, chill out, mate. I just thought I'd save some time on this one!"

"Well, think again, buddy. They don't deserve to ride in the same wagon as our sarge."

He just looked at me and luckily he realised I was completely serious, so they quietly loaded Shelley into the wagon and headed off for the morgue.

With all the formalities complete inside, the big guy strolled out shouting, "Mac, Smithy, let's get them saddled up, it's time to go back to The Rest!"

Smithy's crew loaded into the three-tonner and my wagon leaned over as the large one got in beside me.

He was unusually subdued and all I got from him was a quiet, "Back to The Rest, Mac."

Chapter Twenty-one

A Debt Repaid

I had just returned from a town patrol with Webber, it had been long and boring and uneventful, until the crazies decided to have a pop at us, yet again.

We were both dog tired and the boredom had made things worse. Until I came around a corner and suddenly there in front of us, in the middle of the road, was a Black Balaclava Boy, and the fact that he had an RPG up on his shoulder in the firing position, sent both our adrenalin levels surging sky high.

Instinctively, I wrenched the Land Rover to the right and tramped on the gas pedal just as he fired. The RPG came so close that it left scorch marks down the side of my wagon.

Still with my foot on the floor, I swung back into the middle of the road and bore down on the boy. He stood there transfixed, he had no time to reload, or even get out of my way.

By now I was doing about 35 miles an hour as my front bumper struck him between his knees and his waist with a terrible grinding crunch and he gave out a despairing wail as he went right over the top of my wagon and landed in a heap in the middle of the road, like a pile of discarded rags.

When I finally pulled up with a screech of brakes in the middle of the road, the large one looked at me white faced and shaking, which was most unusual for him.

"Nice driving, Mac," he said. Like me he had a picture in his head of that tank-buster being a few inches to the right, and imagining what it would have done to us and my wagon.

Straight away I called it in to The Rest on the radio so they could get an ambulance on the way, along with a foot patrol to secure the scene.

We both got out very carefully, fully armed and very much wary of another ambush.

When we got back to the crumpled heap in the road, it took only a cursory examination to see that he would not be ambushing anyone else, ever again.

"You all right, Mac?" said Webber. After all, I had just killed a man.

"Hell yes. If I didn't get him, we would be sitting in that Land Rover burnt to a crisp!"

A few minutes later, Sergeant Danny Baker turned up with a five-man patrol and they quickly secured the area.

"Hey, guys. What have you been up to?"

"Hell, Danny, we're just taking care of business," I said.

Then the ambulance turned up and things had changed from the first call. They were no longer an ambulance, they were a meat wagon bound for the morgue.

"Okay, Danny," said Webber. "Have you got this now? We've got a lot of paperwork to do back at The Rest."

"Yeah, go for it, guys," laughed Danny. "We'll clean up your mess."

Then we packed up and headed for The Rest.

I dropped Webber off at the front door and went across to the car park to put my baby to bed, once more with damage, but this time it was only scorch marks down the left-hand side and not bullet holes.

When I went in the front door, Webber said, "Parker wants to see you in his office, Mac."

I thought, oh shit, what have I done now?

I stowed my gear in my room and went back to knock on Parker's door.

"Come in," said Parker, and I opened the door and walked in.

Parker had company and I looked at the young lady sitting there, not recognising her.

I looked askance at the boss and I said, "You wanted me, sir?"

He said, "Actually I didn't. She did," indicating the visitor. So I looked at her, still without recognition.

"Okay. You wanted to speak to me?" I still didn't recognise her, but I thought it can't be that I've got her in trouble. I certainly hadn't done any walking out since I'd been there. In that place it would really be taking a chance.

Then she spoke and the sound of her voice transported me back months to a very bad time.

I had been on a foot patrol in downtown Derry when we had walked into a roadside bomb. In Afghanistan they call it an IED, an improvised explosive device. In Ireland all those years ago we called it a roadside bomb. At the end of the day it was the same thing, and it had the same result.

In this case we lost two men and Sergeant Taylor was CASEVACed to hospital, where after a lot of expert treatment, he survived. I ended up at the bottom of the blast hole with three bullet holes in me and completely flash blind from the bomb blast.

I had never seen her face, but I did know that she saved my life and that I wouldn't be here now if it wasn't for her.

She said, "Do you know me?"

I said, "I know your voice and I haven't forgotten what you have done for me."

"Do you remember what you said when I brought you back here?" she said.

"I remember. I said, if I can ever do anything for you, you only have to ask." I looked at Parker and he nodded in agreement. "Ask away," I said. "Let's see what we can do."

"It's not only me that needs help," she said. "The IRA hardmen have started a training camp on a farm near

Ballymena. But their so-called recruits are not volunteers." Here she started to break down and cry.

"Go ahead," Parker encouraged her.

Eventually she regained control. "They are young boys, between 14 and 18 and they are kidnapped and forced to do the training. Some idealistic young boys obviously don't need to be forced into the weapon training and bomb making, but some, like my little brother Jamie, who is only 14½ don't want anything to do with it! They are kidnapped and forced into it, and they are kept in line with threats against their families."

"What threats?" asked Parker.

"Rape, torture, and murder," she sobbed. By this time Webber had joined us and Parker brought him up to date.

"My God," said Parker. "We have enough trouble with the born and bred diehards without having these youngsters forced into it. This is something I need to take up with the brass. Meantime, you two can start planning a way out of this."

Webber was thinking aloud. "First we need 14 Company on side. We need plenty of intelligence: location, numbers, and arms for a start. Then we need to know exactly where on the farm that these kids are situated at night. I think that would be the best time to give them the good news."

"Well, we can't do anything without the brass on side, and all those details from 14 Company," said Parker.

Then I had to put in my two cents worth. "What about the small soldiers at Rosemount? They're the best guys for a night hit, even the regiment will agree with that."

Parker was all business now. "I'll sort out 14 Company and the brass. You sort out the Gurkhas then we'll have another meeting."

He turned to the young lady. It was safer for her if we kept her name out of it.

"You go home," he said to her. "Leave all this to us. It's best if you stay away now, for your own safety, but we'll keep you informed of our progress."

164

And with that he disappeared into his office to get on with the red tape.

I turned to her. "He's right you know. You will be safer if you stay away. I'll give you the phone number here in case you need to get in touch, but believe me, we'll do the best we can. It's to the army's benefit to get rid of this place as much as that of the families of the kidnapped kids," and with that she was gone.

Webber said, "Parker will do his bit. Let's go up and see the small soldiers."

While he was getting ready and booking us out with the control room, I went across to the car park and got my vehicle ready.

When he came out he had a corporal and two privates with him. Gerry Anderson and Corporal Bill Edwards got into another Land Rover and they were to act as follow car, and Dave Edwards, no relation, got into the back of my wagon to act as vehicle escort.

At that time in Derry, the British Army didn't go anywhere unless they were armed to the teeth and mob handed and they always travelled in convoy, at least two vehicles or more, just in case.

So off we trundled, heading for Rosemount with my wagon in the lead. It was a short trip from The Rest through the town square and up William Street to Rosemount School, only about 15 minutes at the most, and the little guys were expecting us, Webber having sent a radio message from The Rest before we had left. After all, it didn't do to surprise these little mountain men from Nepal, especially after the disturbance up there when the Black Balaclava Boys had hit the Redcaps stationed there and we had sadly lost Dick Shelley. To do that would really be like stirring up a hornet's nest as the boys had found out the hard way when they had foolishly tried to have a go at the small soldiers.

Our little convoy rolled in the gate and we were welcomed, as usual, with beaming smiles and mugs of sweet hot tea.

The happy band of little warriors had already christened Webber "Yeti" for obvious reasons and no matter how hard he tried to hide it, he was delighted.

With Webber and I comfortably seated and the little sergeant standing proudly to attention by the door, Webber started to explain the situation to the diminutive captain.

As his explanation proceeded, the little guys grew more and more delighted.

"We are honoured, Sergeant Major Yeti, that you would choose us for such an important mission."

"Well, Captain Rai, we are well aware of the expertise of your men on night manoeuvres, especially this old Yank here, who has had his bootlaces tied together by your boys in the dark," and this brought smiles of great delight from the little men.

"But on a serious note," said Webber. "There will be hostages at the farm when we hit it and we can't afford to lose any of them. That would enhance their recruiting program to no end."

"I understand," Captain Rai replied. "Will you and Yankee Boy be coming with us?"

Webber wasn't the only one to get a nickname from the little guys.

"We certainly will," grinned Webber. "But we have to gather all the necessary intelligence first, then we will have two or three practice runs in a remote location yet to be decided. If you could select your assault team in the meantime, I suggest a sergeant, a corporal and five or six men, all we can do then is to wait for the relevant intelligence."

"Excellent, Sergeant Major Yeti," smiled the little captain. "You let us know when you are ready and I can assure you that we also will be ready and waiting."

On the way back to The Rest I turned to Webber.

"Damn, sir, these little guys are keen as mustard. We're going to have to be sharp just to keep up with them at night."

"Yes, Mac, you are. I want you to go in with the assault team to secure those kids and look after them. When they see these little guys operate, it's going to be a real shock to their systems!"

"Jesus, boss. When those boys are let loose in the middle of the night, it might even be a shock to *my* system!"

"You know what, Mac? Somehow I just can't believe that," chuckled the large one.

We got back to The Rest and I went to park up while Webber went in to see how Parker had got on with 14 Company and the brass.

When I got back inside, I stashed my gear in my room and I didn't have long to wait for the dull roar from the direction of Parker's office.

Bill Edwards passed by on his way to the canteen.

"Hey, Mac, I think Webber just bellowed for you!"

"Yeah," I laughed. "I think they probably heard him in Belfast!"

I wandered into Parker's office and my ears were immediately assaulted.

"Where've you been, Mac?" he roared. "Major Parker is waiting to give us a progress report!"

I pulled up a chair and sat down. "Okay, boss, shoot." I wasn't about to let the large one get me excited.

"Right," said Parker. "I've run this right up to the top, with the brass and they are really keen to get a good result on this one. How did you get on with the Gurkhas?"

Webber said, "All sorted, sir. Captain Rai was selecting his assault team when we left. As soon as 14 Company come up with the goods, we'll bring the little guys down here for rehearsals, then we'll run through it until I'm happy. Then it will be up to you when we go in. On the night the little guys will do the assault, Mac will go in with them to secure the prisoners while the boys do their stuff, and I'll set up an ambush with a few of our guys, probably a sergeant and four men. Anyone who slips through the assault team's fingers and makes a run for the main road will be mopped up by us, but I don't think we'll be overworked."

Parker said, "Are you all right with that, Mac?"

"Fine, sir," I said. "When do you expect to start getting material from 14 Company?"

"A full team has already been tasked with that job, Mac. I'm expecting reports to start coming in at any time."

Webber said, "I think that's it, sir. As soon as material starts coming in we'll get the assault team in here and start briefings!"

"Okay, Sergeant Major. Choose your ambush team now and brief them as much as you can. As soon as I start to get intel I'll pass it on to you."

The next few days passed slowly with routine duties, mobile patrols, foot patrols, guard duty, road blocks, checkpoints, the occasional riot, all the usual stuff.

One morning after breakfast, Webber bellowed down the hall, "Come on, Mac. We're wanted in the major's office!"

"Right, sir, I'm on my way!"

When we got in the office there was a longhaired bearded geezer dressed in dirty jeans and a scabby old raincoat with a stack of paperwork and photos in front of him.

Parker announced, "This is Captain Davis from 14 Company Intelligence to give us a briefing on the training school. We will call it Green Farm."

"Right, lads," Davis started in, "here we go. This job could be a bit of a shitter. My boys say there will be a sentry with a radio near the junction of the main road and the farm track. He will have to be dealt with before he can get a message off. Then when your assault team approaches the main farmhouse, there will be a roving sentry to be dealt with. There will be five more IRA men in the farmhouse, sleeping, eating, or watching television. They will have to be dealt with next. Then behind the farmhouse you'll find a shitty old barn. There are five hostages in there, with one guard. When this guard is dealt with you'll need someone to look after them." That was me.

"Now believe me, lads, these are all hardcore IRA men, all known to us, and we believe they won't hesitate to kill their hostages if you back them into a corner, which, of course, is exactly what you are going to do!"

At this point Parker piped up and said, "We'll be using Gurkhas on the assault team and we fully expect them to neutralise the IRA men before they have a chance to turn on the prisoners!"

Captain Davis replied, "I really hope so, Major, I really hope so. These kids won't have a chance if they don't."

Before the briefing finished, Parker asked Captain Davis to keep us up to date with intel from the farm, to which he received an enthusiastic affirmative.

"Right, Mac," said Webber. "Time to get the assault team over here and start rehearsals."

"Right, boss. Can we get the armourers to work here? Silenced MP5s and Browning Hi-Power sidearms would be most useful on this job. We are going to be looking for a silent in and out on this, which is what these little guys do best."

"Right, Mac. I'll get on the radio and get the Gurkhas down here and we'll organise rehearsals. Major Parker can organise weapons and up-to-date intel from 14 Company. Also, we need aerial recon so that we can get an accurate layout of the farm as we are going to be working in the dark."

Webbers mind was working at full speed now.

"Mac, I want you to rehearse the assault team until you can actually do it in the dark, and completely silently. If we lose any of these kids, we might as well go back to England and sign on the dole! Come on, Mac, let's get this one just right, for the sake of these kids," he said.

"Come on, boss. You know these little guys are experts at this kind of job."

Then he brightened, "I know, Mac, I'm just frightened for these kids." This was not like Webber at all.

The next day things started to move at a faster pace. Sergeant Limbu and his team moved into The Rest with us and promptly upset our cook by instructing him in the art of preparing a burning hot goat curry.

Captain Davis arrived with the aerial recon photos, which we set up on the large table in the lecture room and we all studied them until we had committed the layout of the farm completely to memory. The tiny sergeant and I went through the routine with the assault team time and time again. We would leave Webber and the ambush team about 500 yards from the junction of the farm track and the main road.

We would move forward until we got to the sentry post on the farm track. The little sergeant would send one of his team and scratch one Black Balaclava sentry. Then we would move on to the farmhouse.

While the small soldiers were finishing off the team in there, I would move on to the barn. I knew I had one man to deal with in there, then it was a case of just looking after the kids until the men in the farmhouse were taken care of. Anyone who escaped the little mountain men would be mopped up by Webber's cut-off team. Easy? Of course it was.

Webber called me into Parker's office.

"Well, Mac, what do you think?"

"I think that we are more than ready, sir, and we should go as soon as possible. The longer we hang about, the longer we wait, the more chance there is that the IRA will get wind of what we are doing. Don't forget that their intel is, after all, pretty good. If we pick a farm like our target and conduct rehearsals there, they will probably get wind of what we are up to. No, I think we should go as soon as possible!"

Parker said, "I'll inform the brass that we're ready on standby to go as soon as we get the all clear."

"Right, Mac, get your small soldiers ready, we'll be off as soon as we get the message from brigade headquarters," said the big shit.

I wandered down to see the little guys and the diminutive Sergeant Hari brightened visibly as I entered the room.

"Hey, Yankee Boy. We are all ready, when do we go?"

I grinned at the excited little sergeant.

"Get them stood by with full arms, ammunition and kit. We are just waiting for a message from HQ then we'll move on out to the transport."

This brought an excited babble of Nepalese from the boys and in no time at all they were ready to move out and were eyeing me expectantly, waiting for the go ahead.

I went to my room and picked up my weapons, ammunition and belt gear. I went back to the little guys and led the way down to the canteen. We would at least be going out with a full stomach.

Webber's ambush team, lead by Sergeant Danny Smith and Corporal Bill Edwards, filed in with full stomachs on their minds as well. After all, we didn't know how long we were going to be out that night.

The good-natured banter got underway almost immediately.

"Hey, Mac. Who are your little friends?"

"Yeah," chirped up Bill Edwards. "A bit young to be out this late at night, aren't they?"

But it was all good natured and only a way off releasing the tension building up for the chaos to come during the night, and they were all fully aware of the ferocious reputation of my little friends.

Soon Webber and Parker came into the canteen and called for silence.

"Okay, guys. We've got the go ahead from HQ. You will be moving out in about an hour, after full dark. And let's not forget how important it is to bring back these hostages safely. Good luck to all of you."

"Just one thing, sir. I hope Captain Davis' men have been pulled out. They really don't want to meet up with my little guys in the dark in the woods."

This brought a ripple of laughter from all assembled, including Parker.

"They'll be pulled out as soon as you lot set off," he chuckled.

An hour later we moved over to the car park to find our transport and the army had really pulled out all the stops on this one; 14 Company had their own transport and drivers.

We found an assortment of raggle-taggle rusty old bangers awaiting us in the car park, the most unmilitary transport I had seen since coming to Derry. But believe me, they only *looked* like old bangers, under the hood it was a different story. They were all souped up V8 engines and they could give anything on the road a serious run for its money. And they also loaned us their highly trained drivers so we could really give anything on the road a serious run.

We were also dressed like the 14 Company guys – old jeans and scruffy shirts. The only thing we didn't have was the long scruffy haircuts of our drivers, but I think we could pass muster for one night. We really didn't look like a military convoy; we didn't want the Black Balaclava Boys to be expecting us.

We moved off in one of the most unmilitary convoys ever to grace the streets of Derry. I soon nodded off, which I usually did when I was being transported anywhere – when I wasn't driving, of course. My little friends, although at first surprised, soon took it all in with their customary good humour.

We soon pulled up at our dropping-off point, about 500 yards from the junction of the main road and the farm track.

I have to admit I was a little bit out of my depth with these little guys in the field at night. Don't get me wrong, I was no slouch at the night manoeuvres; I could lose myself in the shadows quite easily and the boys were always moaning at me for giving them a start when I was out and about in the streets at night. But these little guys were something else.

The little sergeant sent his scouts out about 20 yards in front of us and they quickly blended into the night with ghostly efficiency. We moved about 500 yards through the murky night then the little sergeant stopped me with a touch on the arm.

I still don't know how he knew when his scouts had dealt with the sentry, but he did. Eventually he started me off again with another touch on the arm.

Soon we past a crumpled heap by the side of the road, beside a humming radio set. Scratch one Black Balaclava sentry.

We moved along the track like a party of silent grey shadows, floating wraiths in the night.

In the distance I saw some lights and I once more got the touch on the arm, and once again he sent out the silent, deadly scouts. And again we waited silently till I once more got the light touch on the arm – scratch one more sentry – these boys were positively telepathic.

The assault team moved on to the farmhouse to weave their magic spell and now it was my turn. The little sergeant moved off with his assault team and I was left with, to quote Captain Davis, the shitty old barn. There were large gaps in between the wallboards big enough to allow the bats entrance and exit, and luckily big enough for me to recce the inside of the barn.

I put one eye to one of the bigger gaps and I got an eyeful of five terrified-looking youths and one bored-looking IRA man, who was definitely not expecting any trouble. Hell, he only just about had his eyes open,

Around the front of the barn I found a hayloft door with a hoist and a rope for lifting bales of hay up into the loft. I shinned up the rope and into the loft. When I moved forward to the edge of the loft, I saw below me the five scared-looking kids and the bored-looking soldier of the revolution. Unfortunately, at that moment the frightened boys below spotted me and even though I touched my finger to my lips to shush them, they overreacted and the IRA man below saw the looks on their faces and he turned to see what was affecting them.

So much for trying to take him alive, my silenced MP5 coughed twice and he crumpled to the floor, dead.

I dropped down to the floor of the barn and immediately started to free the frightened boys. They all had their hands fastened behind them with plasticuffs.

I was trying to reassure them that they were safe now, but unfortunately the razor sharp stiletto in my hand wasn't very reassuring, even though I was only using it to cut their bonds.

"Easy boys," I said in my best reassuring voice. "You're safe now. There are some scary little guys out there taking care of the rest of the IRA men, but believe me, they're on our side."

I was just about to cut the third kid's hands free when the front door slammed back and one of the IRA boys rushed in as if the Devil himself was hot on his tail, and come to think of it, he actually was.

The boy was carrying an AK47 and there was no way I could let him cut loose at the kids with that.

On boring days back at The Rest I used to spend hours throwing that stiletto at an old dart board, just to pass the time away, and believe me, that dart board was in tatters.

The boy started to bring his AK up into the firing position and I couldn't allow that. It was entirely a reflex action and the boy let out a gurgling cry as my knife took him in the throat. Then his knees buckled and he folded up in a heap on the floor.

Just then the little sergeant rushed in waving his razor sharp Kukri in the air. Enter the Devil that the boy had been running away from.

"Sorry, Yankee Boy. This one got away."

"Don't worry, Sarge," I said. "How are things going out there?"

"No problem," he said. "All finish now!"

Webber would be most upset; we had left nothing for his cut-off team to do!

I said to the now thoroughly frightened kids, "This is Sergeant Hari. He's one of those scary little guys I was talking about. But don't worry, he's definitely on our side! Sarge, if it's all secure out there, you can call in the Yeti and his team and our transport in."

About an hour passed and then I heard vehicles outside. Sergeant Hari sent two of his team in.

I said, "Look after these kids, guys. I'm just going outside to see Sergeant Major Yeti."

When I got outside, Webber was taking over proceedings.

"Hey, Mac. You guys didn't leave anything for us to do!"

"Yeah, you know how keen these little guys are."

Then he was all business again. "Right. Transport's on its way. My ambush team will secure the farm till the clean-up is completed. The meat wagon is on its way and the RUC will be here shortly to take charge of your kids. As soon as the 14 Company taxi drivers are here, take your team back to The Rest. And, Mac. Good job well done. We've had no casualties, and most importantly, the kids are okay!"

I was still wondering how the 14 Company boys would react to being called taxi drivers.

When our scruffy looking 14 Company transport dropped us back at The Rest, we filed in, handed in weapons and gathered in the canteen.

The little guys were happily chattering away when Parker and Webber came in.

Parker started the ball rolling. "We thank you men for a job well done. The kids have been sent back to their very grateful families and there were no casualties at all for us!"

Webber got up and said, "It's been a great honour working closely with our Gurkha friends and we are really looking forward to our next job together."

With that, the little sergeant had his men on their feet standing to attention chanting, "Yeti! Yeti! Yeti!"

Just then the duty signaller came into the noisy room and waved for my attention, miming a phone call. As soon as I heard the hushed voice on the phone I knew who it was.

"How is he?"

She replied, "The doctors say he is physically fine, but will take some time before his mind is healed, though."

"Tell him from me, no thanks are necessary. It is, after all, a debt repaid."

Chapter Twenty-two

Going Home

Our tour in the Province was coming to an end. Finally it was time for the Green Jackets to take over from us in the streets of Derry. We were going back to England, which was home to Webber and the boys, but not to me.

I had come to England and joined the British Army and was posted immediately to the madness of the Province in turmoil in the late '60s. I had never experienced the barrack duty of a home posting in England and if I was honest with myself, I really didn't know if I could do it. I had come here to get away from the general and my worst nightmare would be to go back to Seattle and that old tyrant. Anything but that, so I really didn't have a home to go to. Webber and I had talked long into the night on this very subject and I know he was worried what my final decision would be. It wasn't just a matter of giving me promotion, he knew how I felt about that. Promotion was of absolutely no interest to me.

The boys were all on a high to be going home to England, to a long leave and then back to boring mundane barrack duties. But I still didn't know if I could settle for that. I suppose there was always the dirty jobs for Box that I had been offered by the slimy suit when I was banished to Akrotiri Airbase after a particularly nasty "wet job" in Derry, but I really couldn't see myself doing that.

We were going back to England and leaving behind the memories of friends, body bags, the sometimes bad times, sometimes good times we'd had there, and memories of friends like Dick Shelley, who wouldn't be coming back to England with us because he was already there in his home town, in a cold, cold grave.

The rest of us would go back to England on a car ferry across the Irish Sea. Three-tonners, pigs, our affectionate name for the pug-ugly but lifesaving Saracen armoured cars, and our old thin-skinned Land Rovers, because we were too early for the heavy-duty grey armoured Land Rovers to be introduced later. Men, weapons and equipment, all loaded on an old roll-on, roll-off. And to say that we all gathered in the bar for celebratory drinks would be an understatement. Well, we had something to celebrate after all, we had made it.

We would go back on our own two feet, some of us with scars and bullet holes; some like Webber, with his wasted, half-plastic face, a souvenir of a gunfight on the Craigavon Bridge. But we had all learned to live with pain, either the physical pain from the various wounds we would carry on our bodies, or the mental pain, some of it leading to severe cases of PTSD.

The memory of the trip back is still with me after all these years.

The memory of the piss-up in the bar of the ferry on the way back to England; the memory of a drunken private climbing the mast in a force nine gale, and the officers and NCOs saying, "Oh, they're only blowing off steam. They've earned it" is still with me after all these years.

Webber came into the bar, into the chaos that was in full flow, and the crowd of drunken, staggering, sweaty bodies parted for him as if by magic, like Moses parting the Red Sea, such was the respect that these drunken, celebrating men had for this 300lb man mountain.

He spotted me sitting in a corner all by myself, working on a pint of warm beer and a large vodka. When in England for any length of time, you get used to warm beer.

His wasted face creased into a broad grin and he turned back to the bar. Soon he returned to my table bearing a tray with two pints and two large vodkas on it.

I couldn't help but smile when he sat down. I said, "Shit, sir. You'll get a bad reputation sitting in the enlisted men's bar drinking with a lowly private."

He chuckled and said, "Tonight you can just stop calling me sir. And while I stick two fingers up at the brass, we can get stuck in starting work on a massive hangover."

I said, "Shit, man. You'll get me a bad name. You know what they said in Nam? You Brits have a drink problem and us Yanks have a drug problem!"

"Fuck 'em, old friend. You don't have a drug problem and after all we've been through, we deserve a drink."

The ferry was now into serious rolling due to the force nine gale that we were in and I said, "What about the boy up the mast?"

"Oh shit, there's enough officers on the boat to deal with him. But we've got some serious drinking to do and if we don't get off of this rowboat with a serious hangover in the morning, I will be reporting both of us for gross dereliction of duty!"

I couldn't stop myself from bursting into laughter, "Then in that case you'd better tell that waiter to keep them coming," and I threw a £20 note on the table and the large one did the same, and waved the waiter over.

"Just keep going till that lots gone," he growled. "Me and my friend here have some serious drinking to do, and by the way, son," he said, catching the worried boy's arm, "we'll buy you a drink in this round, but we don't expect to be buying you any more tonight. Understand me?"

"Yes, sir. Sorry, sir," stuttered the worried-looking waiter as he scuttled off to get our drinks.

I just sat there with a silly grin on my face till the frightened little waiter returned with our drinks.

I said, "Do you think that the fact that you have a face that's half plastic and your bridgework has been rebuilt with stainless steel after our little gunfight on the Craigavon Bridge might have something to do with this marvellous service we are getting tonight?"

This brought another gust of laughter from him and he roared, "Not a bit of it!"

"Anyway," I laughed with him. "You know I don't know what to call you if I can't call you sir."

This brought another gust of laughter. "And what about all those other names you guys call me when you think I can't hear you, like large one, or big shit? Need I go on?"

I said, "Whatever do you mean, sir?"

And to this he just laughed and said, "Why don't you call me Irving, Yank."

I nearly choked on my drink, "Irving?"

He said, "Well, that's my first name. What's yours?"

And with drunken soldiers all around us, I had to man up and admit my name was George Washington Mallory and now it was the big shit's turn to choke on his drink.

He spluttered, "Did I hear you right, Yank?"

I laughed, "Well, what can I say, Irving. The general was a very patriotic man."

The big guy put his glass in the air for me to clink with him and he said with a rumbling laugh, "Well, come on, George Washington, we've got some serious drinking to do!"

And all I could do was to clink glasses with him and try to keep up and not get left by the wayside.

I said, "You know what, Irving? You've got the advantage on me straight away with body mass. You weigh in at about 300lbs, at least!"

He laughed and said, "Three twenty, actually. But forget about body mass, you've had enough practice by now to keep up with me." Then he let go with the rumbling laugh that he was famous for. "Come on, George, we've got some drinking to do!"

"Skol!" I said, raising my glass.

"Dosvadanya!" roared the big bugger, raising his glass and draining it. Shit, I thought, keeping up with him was going to be harder than I thought.

After a couple of hours of "Slangevar", "Prosit", "Good Luck", "Bottoms Up", and all that, the big shit suddenly said, "Look, Mac, I know that you're worried about what the regiment will do next, but do me a favour, will you? Don't make any decision until after disembarkation leave and we know what's next on the agenda. We can't afford to lose you."

I just couldn't resist a sly dig here. "Why, Irving," I laughed. "I really didn't know you cared."

And 300-plus pounds of sergeant major growled, "Don't push your luck, Yank! But he just couldn't hold the threat and he dissolved into laughter and poured another pint down his throat.

Just them a scuffle broke out between a sapper who had been attached to us and one of our Three Platoon bods.

Webber got out of his chair and with all the dignity he could muster, said, "Excuse me, my friend, I will be right back."

He pushed his way through the crowd of soldiers, shouting, "Fight! Fight! Fight!" When he arrived at the scene of the push and shove contest, he didn't even speak to them, he just latched to the collar of each of the protagonists and hoisted them unceremoniously off the floor. He then proceeded across the dance floor with two fairly large men dangling with their toes barely touching the floor and deposited them on the small stage and once more with dignity, stated, "Right, you two assholes. If you are going to insist on making a spectacle of yourselves, you can do it on the stage and provide the night's entertainment for the rest of us."

At which point the whole bar dissolved once more into laughter at the two red-faced idiots on the stage and then we all got on with the business at hand, which was making sure we drank the whole ferry dry.

At around 2030 hours, the officer of the day, a young first Louie of the rather posh kind, showed up in the bar to check on the bedlam in progress. The young lad really didn't know what he was doing wrong when he marched up to Webber and snootily informed him that he was in the wrong bar. The whole room fell into deathly silence as we eagerly awaited the outcome of his *faux pas*, and even though it was the result of his being greener than the vegetables in the kitchen, none of us were going to help the poor lad out, as we eagerly awaited the outcome of the next instalment in the night's entertainment.

Webber, still with the complete dignity of the not quite drunk, sat there regarding the lad with a smile on his face. Then he said, "Listen and learn, Lieutenant Jameson," I was surprised that he even remembered the boy's name, but by now nothing about Webber should have surprised me.

The boys gathered around our table, awaiting the forthcoming explosion with bated breath, but it never came.

The next person through the door happened to be Major Parker, who surveyed the room, spotted our table, and, taking in the scene with a glance and no doubt noticing Webber's reddening face, marched over to our table and pulled out a chair and sat down, much to the amazement of the young lieutenant, who was still hovering over us.

He then picked up an unattached pint and promptly drained half of it. Then smacking his lips, he said, "Evening, Sergeant Major, evening, Mac." Much to the amazement of the young lieutenant and then he waved to our even-more-flustered waiter and ordered a round of drinks for the table.

Well, the young lieutenant was so amazed that when his wide open mouth finally snapped shut, all he could do was shake his head in amazement and quickly vacate the bar.

Things instantly returned to normal and the background roar of laughter and conversation returned, even though most of the boys were disappointed that the promised entertainment had never materialised.

"How goes the celebration guys?" chuckled Parker, well aware of the impending confrontation that he had just thwarted.

"We're getting there, sir," rumbled Webber. "Have another drink, sir," and all this still with the utmost dignity of the almost drunk.

Parker laughed and said, "Well, I think I'd be pushing my luck. It wouldn't be safe for me to stay and drink with you reprobates."

Webber said, "By the way, sir. Did you know that our resident Yank was thinking of leaving us when we get back to England? He thinks there won't be enough happening to stop him getting bored. I've convinced him to stay till after disembarkation leave, but that's as far as he'll commit."

Parker, well aware of my opinions on promotion, didn't even bother to offer it, but he did say, "Stick around, Mac, we can always find something for someone of your special talents."

I said, "Yeah, that's what that slimy spook from Box said when I was in Cyprus. But I don't trust them."

Parker said, "But you know that you can trust us," and I couldn't argue with that. I could only smile and nod at the pair of them.

With that, Parker drained his glass and laughed. "Now I'm going to get out of here before you lot get me in trouble. I want the captain of the ferry to come to me and tell me you lot drank his ship dry." To me he said, "Stick with us, Mac. Give us a chance. I'll assign a driver to your Land Rover in the morning, I don't want you capable of driving."

and we both raised our glasses to him, and the boys raised a ragged cheer to him as he left.

Webber stood up and raised his glass to the assembly and roared, "Once more into the breach, you motley crew, and once more drained his glass to tumultuous applause from aforesaid motley crew.

Just then the door slammed back and in trooped eight of the little smiley guys that had been working with us since the sad time at Rosemount School when we lost Dick Shelley. It was Sergeant Hari Limbu and some of his happy band of small soldiers. Shit, now we were in for a party; these little guys liked their beer and they were not worried about body mass; they had a lot less than us, after all.

"Hey, Yankee Boy, Yeti," shouted the little sergeant. "Any party here?"

"Yeti" was their affectionate name for Webber and he pretended to hate it but couldn't hold the scowl. He loved the nickname and he had every respect for these hard little fighting men from the mountains of Nepal.

"Damn, there sure is now," he roared in his dulcet tones. "Pull up some more chairs, boys," making the little guys grin from ear to ear with pure delight.

When they were all seated, the diminutive sergeant threw his hat on the table and threw a £10 note in it, and we all followed suit. Webber bellowed for our previously worried waiter, who was now looking positively terrified.

When the waiter finally got the table piled high with drinks and once more retreated to the neutral safety of the bar, the party got well and truly underway. Our table was quickly turning into the most interesting in the room, due mainly to the presence of the little guys and the Yeti, so more and more tables were pulled together as our ranks swelled.

The Gurkhas treated us to a display of their martial arts drill with the world famous "Kukri", the most deadly close-quarter weapon used by any soldiers in the world.

With the amount of alcohol being consumed at the time, it was a minor miracle no one parted company with their heads, which after all was the purpose of the Kukri in the first place. But a good time was had by all and the only blood spilt was from the solemn pricking of a finger to satisfy the tradition of the blade tasting blood before it could once more be sheathed.

The night progressed, the drink flowed and the little guys started to chant for Webber to do a turn.

The cry went up, "Yeti! Yeti! Yeti!" and the big guy finally raised his arms for silence, and when he solemnly tried to climb on the table to do a dance, we had to convince him it was a bad idea as the table would never have taken his weight.

Eventually he conned me into doing the Egyptian sand dance with him and the small soldiers were beside themselves in rapturous delight; they nearly brought the house down chanting "Yeti!" and "Yankee Boy!"

A guy from Three Platoon treated us to a piano recital on the old upright piano in the bar and then accompanied us in a good old knees-up sing song, which also stirred the little guys to heights of rapturous applause.

Around midnight, they all lapsed suddenly into a solemn silence and we all wondered what was coming next.

Just then the door opened and their Captain Shailendra Rai entered solemnly, followed by three white-clad waiters wheeling vast colanders of the famous and fiery Gurkha goat curry, so loved by these fierce little mountain men. They solemnly passed a bowl to everyone who would have one, which most of the men took, after all, it was a good excuse to drink copious draughts of ale soon after to try and drown the fire in your belly when you can be forgiven for thinking you are losing your stomach lining.

Everyone was busy chewing on goat curry and drinking gallons of beer, when the little captain gave his sergeant a wave, who promptly jumped up on the table shouting for silence, his captain was about to make a speech.

When bedlam was finally silenced, the little guy solemnly said, "We make many new friends here on this tour. But we want to honour two special friends," then once again they began to chant, "Yeti! Yankee Boy!"

And they wouldn't stop until we were on our feet in front of the whole assembly, where they solemnly presented us with a beautiful silver inlaid ceremonial Kukri each.

And unbelievably, even the large one was lost for words. Although only momentarily. After all, he was the Yeti.

After we had both said our thanks to them, the party resumed at full bore, getting louder and louder as it progressed. Then Webber called me into a corner.

"Jesus, Mac, what are we going to do about this? We need to find something to give to the little guys in return."

I said, "Hell, Irving, I don't know. I wasn't expecting this any more than you were, but we have to give them something."

Suddenly he brightened. "Hell, I know just what to give them. Keep things going here, Mac. I'll be right back."

He was gone about 15 minutes, when he came back into the bar and the cry once more went up around the bar, and this time it wasn't only the little guys chanting, "Yeti! Yeti! Yeti!" Our guys were just as loud as the Gurkhas.

He had a polished wooden presentation case under his arm and when I looked closer at it, I could see he had removed a plaque from the front of the box. I said, "What's going on, Irving?" I had no Idea what he was up to.

"Whatever happens, play along with me, Mac," and he stood up to make an announcement, after calling for silence and eventually getting it.

"Unaccustomed as I am to public speaking," he started off – a joke that was lost on the Gurkhas, as it went straight over their heads, not translating at all, but eventually he managed to get to the point.

I had never seen Webber lost for words, but he very nearly was then. When the boys had finally got the little captain standing there by the Yeti, he finally got around to saying, "Mac and I were very grateful for our presents earlier on, and although your present wasn't ready then, it certainly is now, and we are proud to present our Gurkha friends with…well, this," as he stumbled over the last words.

Then he opened the box and I was just as gobsmacked as the little guys when I finally got a look inside. It was my old Beretta and silencer, a souvenir of my time as the smelly one from the streets. But when I took a second look, I saw it wasn't really the same gun. Webber had got the armourers working overtime on it and the gun was a sight to see. Blued, polished and engraved to perfection, it was now a beautiful presentation model.

When I saw the little captain's face, all I could think was, although it was my gun, it was certainly worth losing it to see the little guys gazing at it in complete wonderment, and then to hear them ensuring Webber it would find a place of honour in their museum back at Maidstone Barracks.

When the big guy finally sat down at the table beside me again, he said, "Sorry, Mac. That was meant for you when we got back to England."

I said, "I had no idea you still had it. I thought it would be at the bottom of the Irish Sea by now."

"It was meant to be a surprise for you when we got back to England," he said.

I said, "Don't worry, Irving. Just to see the looks on their faces made it all worthwhile. Now let's get on with drinking this scow dry." And that's just what we did.

This night was to pass into regimental legend. Not least because I left the party draped over Webber's shoulder, out like a light, or so they told me anyway. God, I would never live it down.

All I can remember was waking up in the back of my Land Rover and when I managed to lift my pounding head over the level of the front seat, I found Webber in the passenger seat and young Smithy driving.

Webber handed me a coke and a handful of paracetamol with a roaring laugh. But all I could do was to point out the window and gape with amazement. There were three pigs abreast, barrelling down the M1 having a race.

"Yeah," shrugged the large one. "The boys got a bit bored with all this convoy driving. Go back to sleep, you old bastard. We'll wake you up when we get back to barracks," and all I could do was to shake my head in amazement, a real mistake with a headache like mine. I really needed to beat a strategic retreat back into sleep again.

"Time for a pitstop," I grated. I still had a gravel pit in my throat in spite of the coke I had downed with the paracetamol.

"No pitstop, Yank," roared the big shit with a laugh. "Can't stop the convoy for you!"

Oh well, I thought, needs must come first and all that. So I stood up at the back of the Land Rover, pulled back the canvas cover and let fly. This brought a delighted laugh from the big guy as he shouted, "Don't fall out the back, you daft old bastard!"

Mind you if I had, it would have at least cured my raging headache.

There were no civilian cars coming past to see what I was up to and the only reaction from the next vehicle in line, apart from dropping back accordingly to increase the spacing, was a lot of pointing and laughing.

I shouted, "In my defence, it's damn cold back here!" but I doubt if they would have stopped laughing even if they heard me.

Finally we pulled up in Chattenden Barracks, the Gurkhas having split off from the convoy and headed for Maidstone.

Here we were at the end of one chapter and the beginning of another in my life. I still didn't know what my next step would be yet, but I had promised Webber that I wouldn't make a decision until after disembarkation leave, I owed the big bugger that much. But somehow I couldn't see this being the end of the road for us. There had to be more to come.

The End

Glossary

SLR – 7.62mm self-loading rifle.

SMG – 9mm Sterling sub-machine gun.

GPMG – 7.62mm general purpose machine gun. The replacement for the much loved Bren gun. The GPMG wasn't well accepted when first introduced, notably when it was issued to the SAS in Indo China, where they were promptly dumped in a river and they politely requested the return of their Bren guns.

RPG – Rocket propelled grenade. A hand-held anti-tank weapon that has been around for years and has been used all over the world by terrorist groups to great effect, notably the Provisional IRA.

Carl Gustav – The modern equivalent of the bazooka, another hand-held anti-tank weapon.

Canadian Browning Hi-Power – 9mm, semi-automatic pistol on issue to the British Army for many years.

Pig – Six-wheeled APC (armoured personnel carrier) used widely in Northern Ireland.

Prestel – The button on the top of the Pioneer radio mike that you need to press to send a message.

81mm mortar – The modern replacement for the old 3" mortar, used to great effect in the deserts of Oman, Dhofar and Aden, or South Yemen, as it is now called.

Wessex – The big old lumbering workhorse helicopter that saw widespread service back in the '60s and 70s in the desert theatres and then as coastguard search and rescue back in England, and also in the Falklands War.

Wasp – A small two-man helicopter fitted with baskets across the struts to make a CASEVAC vehicle that saved many lives and were a welcome sight buzzing into many an awkward situation, in many theatres.

CASEVAC – Short for 'Casualty Evacuation'.

Baton Rounds – The infamous and devastating rubber bullets that could knock the stuffing out of the most dedicated rioter in a matter of seconds. Still on issue to the army and police today.

Sit-rep – Situation report.

The Regiment – Our name for the SAS.

14 Company Intelligence – Out in the streets, mixing with the IRA and the UVF, they had one of the most dangerous jobs undertaken by the British Army in Ulster.